SUNSET
BE GLORY

England's smugglers are in dire straits as the clock ticks off the final minutes of the 18th century before the birth of the 19th. Richard John, a self-made man who has become a living legend in North Yorkshire and County Durham, has spent his life forging an empire built on illegally importing and distributing liquor. Now in his sixties he realises his career no longer yields excitement nor satisfaction. With an eye on retirement, he discovers his son Tom refusing to take over the family business, and his daughter Margaret just as headstrong, shrugging off any attempt to encourage her to settle into domestic bliss. With the authorities closing in, determined to stamp out the contraband trade, Richard John suddenly finds himself fighting for his way of life.

Then he meets Valentine Rudd.

SUNSET
BE GLORY

CHRIS SCOTT WILSON

seaside
BOOKS

First published by Seaside Books 2016

©2000/2016 C.J.S. Wilson

ISBN 978-0-9508631-6-0

Contact : seasidebooks@outlook.com

author website : www.chrisscottwilson.co.uk

cover design by Eddie Guy at Signart
printed by Bob Watson at Quoin.

SUNSET
BE GLORY

ONE

"If you can't see anything, pass the glass."

Roland Flounder's voice hissed like wind through dry summer grass. He snatched the telescope from Valentine Rudd's unwilling hands then screwed up his eyes as he raked the place where the sky should meet the North Sea. Thick cloud obscured the moon just as planned, but sighting the lugger was all the more difficult.

"And what can you see?" Valentine asked with a sneer, confident Roland's eyes were no better than his own. Sometimes his partner's all too knowing attitude irritated him. They almost looked the same; three inches short of six feet, strong in arm and stockily built, with long unruly brown hair that curled round long faces. They also had the same brown eyes that watched the world around hawkish noses above almost identical lantern jaws. And yet they were completely different. For as many generations as they could remember, Roland Flounder's family had been agricultural labourers for a succession of tenant farmers on the cliffs above Saltburn, all the children born to live in tied cottages in the hamlet by the shore.

In contrast, Valentine Rudd's family was of the sea. The tides seemed to regulate the pulsing of blood in their veins. On nights when big storm driven rollers crashed up the beach, no male Rudd could sleep soundly, tossing and turning in bed, almost as if the churning ocean also disturbed long forgotten memories of Rudd ancestors battling through typhoons in the China Sea or Jamaica hurricanes, ploughing through the Roaring Forties or weathering Cape Horn, or even the more familiar North-

Easters on the Yorkshire coast which every Rudd knew all too well.

Valentine peered at Roland. Always so sure of himself. Tonight, Valentine's own uncertainty was a snake of fear that uncoiled restlessly in his gut. He stared into the darkness, listening to the waves breaking below, hissing and sucking at the shingle at the beach's edge. They had the best view of the bay, perched a few feet below the crown of Cat Nab which poked up from the shore some sixty feet into the sky like an extinguished volcano of soft clay.

Below, along the fringe of the beach ran a row of cottages, woodsmoke from dying evening fires homely in the night air. To their left the shamble of pantiled roofs petered out where Saltburn beck emerged from the woods to slice across the sand to the sea. Beyond, a cart track twisted up the west cliff into a patchwork quilt of fields belonging to Rifts Farm. Spring crops waved uncertainly above the tumbling slopes of the sea banks running some three miles to Marske above broad sands as flat as a mirror where it was said lords from Skelton Castle used to race their chaises, hooves pounding the damp sand at low tide.

On the other side, their right, where Cat Nab swooped down to the east, yellow squares of light still glowed from the Ship Inn, the breeze-blown sign groaning like a stubborn donkey. Beyond, another ragged line of cottages perched on climbing slopes, standing guard over the tiny crescent of white sand which ended in a solid rock wall. Huntcliff rose sheer, a lion's paw resting on the North Sea, curving protectively round Saltburn Bay. The cliff's sentinels, a horde of screaming cormorants and herring gulls were squeezed onto impossible ledges to roost out the night until the grey dawn started another day's never ending hunt for food.

"I can't see a ..."

His voice died as Valentine's hand chopped sideways for silence. He cocked his head, straining to distinguish the sound again over the tumbling surf. "Someone's coming."

Both lay tense, Roland's hand stealing to the dagger thrust in his belt. Valentine tapped his shoulder and pointed to the right. A man was climbing Cat Nab toward them, stumbling over the rough grass, something large hanging from his right hand. Valentine cupped a hand about his mouth in mime. Roland's teeth gleamed for a second in the darkness as he grinned. Silently, they pressed close to the damp earth, invisible on the hillside.

Valentine lay motionless, the salt breeze in his nostrils. He loved the sea. Back at least to his great-great-grandfather, the Rudds had been fishermen or merchant mariners. Either way they had scoured a living from the sea, and the present generation, he and his father, supplemented that hard earned income on nights like tonight, helping to bring ashore the tubs of brandy and geneva. If his step-mother discovered he was out on the Nab, keeping watch for the smuggling, she wouldn't hesitate to flay him with her tongue, making life a misery. But the men knew. Women did not understand these things. It was something he had to do. It was exciting and he thrived on that excitement. But there was fear too...

Valentine shrugged his thoughts aside and concentrated on the present. Below on the flank of Cat Nab, the newcomer was silhouetted against the indigo sky. He climbed on, grunting with effort, lungs wheezing. He stopped, uncertain, then began to quarter the seaward face of the Nab, searching.

Valentine waited until he came within a yard, then signalled. Roland made a trumpet of his hands, shattering the night with the shriek of a startled owl.

The stranger, startled, staggered sideways. "What the...?"

Valentine lunged upward, grabbed and dragged him down into the grass. "You make enough noise to wake the dead, Tommy."

The newcomer stopped struggling. "For God's sake, Val, you

s-s-scared me. It's not f-f-funny," Tommy Tiplady stuttered. "Mr John wouldn't be happy if he knew you was fooling around when there's work to be done."

"Shut up, Tommy," Roland said.

"You took your time fetching that lantern," Valentine accused. "What if we'd spotted her before you got back? Mr John would have taken his crop to you then." After a moment's silence he added: "You'd best light and cover it, so it's ready. What's happening down there?" He gestured towards the Ship Inn.

Tommy rummaged in a pocket of his threadbare frockcoat for tinderbox and flint, holding the storm lantern between his knees. "The ponies are ready in the yard. The men are in the bar, waiting on Mr John's word."

Valentine could easily imagine the scene. He had witnessed it before. Nobody messed up Mr John's plans. Any hesitation or mistake would be punished by exclusion from the next few runs, and that could mean the difference between eating and starving, the way the fish were running this season. Mr Richard John was as near a perfectionist as any man Valentine had ever met. And his care in planning and flair for organisation had made him rich. So the stage was set. Men and ponies were ready. Soon the message would be carried along the pannier paths to villages far inland.

"John's cow has calfed," it would say…

TWO

"Lights off the port bow," the first mate pointed. "Send word to the Captain." As the cabin boy turned to go below, the mate checked the chart in the dim glow of the binnacle. He nodded, unconsciously shifting his weight to compensate as the *Morgan Butler* rolled beneath his feet to the rhythm of the inshore swell. He glanced up at the sails, grey in the gloom and fat with wind as they drove her westward along a parallel course to the shore. "Tighten that brace!" he called then turned to the helmsman. "Take her two points north; the tide's pulling her in."

"I like a cautious man," a voice growled, then chuckled. "When needs must."

"Good evening to you, Cap'n," the mate smiled, twisting to look over his shoulder as Josiah Brown closed the companion hatchway.

"And a profitable one, too," Captain Brown added with a grin, looking for'ard to take in his lugger's condition all in one practised glance. *Morgan Butler's* transom lifted, timbers creaking, masts swinging in a lazy arc as a shorebound wave rushed beneath her keel to leave a trail of white froth bubbling from her forefoot. Then her bowsprit began the swing toward the open sea, obeying the helmsman's adjustment. Ashore, the cluster of lights slid onto the stern quarter.

"Skinnengrave," the mate offered unnecessarily, well aware his commander knew the Yorkshire coastline so well he could sail it blindfold, smelling his way from harbour to harbour.

"Aye t'is, well enough," Captain Brown agreed. He had large dark eyes below bushy eyebrows, and his strong jutting jawline gave him a stubborn determined look, a dangerous man to cross. When he glowered he conjured the illusion of enough strength to splinter a marline spike with his bare hands. But within seconds, a wicked gleam could spark in his eyes and his laughter would roll forth, as jovial as the landlord of an inn.

Which in a way he was, every square inch of cargo space aboard *Morgan Butler* crammed with more hard liquor than most landlords had ever stored in their cellars. Row upon row of half-ankers of brandy and gin were packed stave to stave, each holding four and a half gallons, nearly 700 of them. Corners were stuffed with extra luxuries, bolts of lace and silk, plus bales of tobacco for good measure. And all worth a fortune once he had landed them safely ashore.

If grave risks were taken, then the rewards justified each and every one. Brown's familiarity with the coastline extended north from the river Humber to Tynemouth. The *Morgan Butler* ran into almost every port, and a few deserted beaches between, and all under the guidance of Richard John. While Captain Brown bought and loaded the cargoes on the continent, Richard John distributed and sold the produce in England. Captain Brown was well along the road to becoming rich. He would have already been wealthy if the government men had minded their own business and let him get on with his.

Not that they frightened him. He had fought both Customs and Excise men on sea and land, and had broken a few heads in the process, his only loss the occasional cargo. But those losses wiped out much of the profits. Once, drinking in a hostelry in Stockton after running in a mixed cargo, half legal and half illegal, he had been asked if he was wary of the King's Officers. He had merely bared his teeth in a wicked grin and tapped the two pistols pushed into his waistband. A man had laughed: "Oh, you trust to God, then?" "God?" Brown had answered. "No, not God. Macham and Macham." When the questioner frowned, Brown had pulled free a pistol and displayed the brass plate on the butt. "Macham and Macham, best gunsmiths in Holland!"

The last two runs had been quiet, and the only sightings since loading at Flushing in Holland had been colliers, scurrying south to feed London's hearths with winter coals. But Captain Brown knew that nothing in the contraband business ran smoothly for long.

"Have the swivel guns loaded," he ordered. "Huntcliff is right up ahead." He squinted into the darkness, trying to discern the outline of the cliff against the sky, but failed. "With the tide making there'll be cross currents. Put a leadsman in the chains both port and starboard. Once we've weathered the point we'll be running into the shallows." He glanced casually into the darkness ahead, then at clouds scudding across the moon. "And stand by to shorten sail."

"Aye aye, sir."

He peered aloft again. No navigation lights tonight. The mainsail was beginning to luff, edges rippling as *Morgan Butler* came more into the wind. Then a current seized her. The bowsprit swung away to port, landwards. Brown turned to bellow but the helmsman was already compensating. Now they would have to see if she obeyed her rudder.

Suddenly the moon was clear, a path of silver gleaming across the sea to reveal a solid wall of black cliffs. And closer than he thought they'd be. Breakers were smashing at their foot, spray climbing and tumbling back. The lugger was dwarfed as she sped toward danger. Five minutes was perhaps all they had. It was no time for mistakes.

"Helm hard a-weather!" Josiah Brown shouted.

"Aye aye, Cap'n," the helmsman grunted, spokes blurring as the wheel spun.

The captain tore his eyes from the cliff and began to spit a steady stream of orders. Bare feet slapped on the decking as men ran for the halyards and braces. "Get those headsails round!"

"God, what a landfall," the mate moaned, staring at the looming cliff.

Josiah Brown scowled. "Huntcliff. All three hundred feet of it. Many a fine vessel has had her ribs stove against those evil rocks." Beneath their feet *Morgan Butler* shivered and groaned, her rudder fighting the hands of wind and tide straining to drive her ashore.

The lugger began to respond, listing as she swung to stand seaward. Tension drained from the mate's voice. "Huntcliff'll not get us tonight. We'll weather her now." The two men both stared over the lee rail as Huntcliff faded into the gloom, clouds once more obscuring the moon. "Do we follow the cliff right round into the bay, Cap'n?"

Brown shook his head. "No, there's a shelf at the foot called Saltburn Scar that runs the best part of a thousand feet out to sea, and westward for another two thousand feet into the bay. We skirt the edge in about three fathoms then run in straight toward the signal light." He looked away from the fading threat of Huntcliff. "Mark!" he called. "Starboard side!"

Standing at the mainchains where the mast ratlines ended in eyebolts on the outer hull, a leadsman leaned out. His weighted line splashed into dark water. As it sank he counted the knots running through his fingers. He marked eight.

"Eight fathoms!"

Too many. Brown scowled. "Portside! Mark!"

"Five fathoms!"

Brown relaxed. They must be on the lip of a hole, the starboard side above it. Charts he had drawn himself gave five fathoms all along this course. With *Morgan Butler* drawing seven feet, they needed to stay in at least three fathoms to retain a safety margin.

"Starboard! Mark!"

"Four!"

The following calls were all five, which brought a grim smile.

No captain liked shoaling water, especially one who could be caught aground with a hold full of contraband liquor. But the only way in to the beach was by risking grounding, and the longer he stayed in the lee of Huntcliff the less likely he was to be seen by prying eyes.

Morgan Butler stole through the night, all hands listening to the waves smashing against the rocks at Huntcliff's foot. Balanced again, the rigging sang a taut melody while the North Sea hissed along the hull. Like sailing through a curtain, a spangle of lights began to twinkle in the night on the port quarter. The mate already held the signalling lantern, gate closed so no light could escape. He looked enquiringly at the captain.

"Not yet." Brown was staring at the lights, calculating how far they had sailed from the cliff. He reckoned they were still above Saltburn Scar, its teeth scant feet from gnawing her hull. Experience selected the lights of the Ship Inn, four square rectangles of yellow painted in the midnight sky. That too was a signal in itself. They seemed to grow no closer as *Morgan Butler* began to wallow as the wind veered. The swell seemed a touch heavier too. Growing. Josiah Brown knew how evil the groundswell could be at Saltburn. On one trip he'd been forced to stand off for four days after abandoning a discharge. *Morgan Butler* had held her ground but the fishing boats'd had a hard time getting off from the beach and back through the surf after each precious cargo had been ferried ashore. Tonight, he reasoned, there should be plenty of time before the swell disrupted operations. He checked the inn's lighted windows again.

"Make the signal."

The mate balanced the lantern on the rail, then quickly opened and closed the gate three times. After a moment the same pattern was repeated by a distant spark, above and to the right of the Ship Inn. "There it is," the mate said.

"Now make four flashes." He watched the mate work, then

counted two in reply. Captain Brown grinned. "Coast's clear. Go for'ard and get the hatch covers off. I'm taking her in."

* * *

The black mare tossed her head, yellow teeth bared as she backed, stamping in the loose box. She snorted, nostrils flared, jerking her muzzle forward, threatening. The bolt rattled then the half door opened and she lunged, lantern light glinting on the steel shoe of her left forefoot as she kicked.

The man laughed as he nimbly side-stepped the flashing hoof, slipping inside in a well practised movement. As the horse's head swung, jaws snapping, he deftly eased the bridle over her ears, slotting the bit between the animal's teeth. The mare admitted defeat, trembling on all four legs, grunts of frustration and anger turning to pleasure as her ears and neck were rubbed, fingers probing and smoothing haunches and legs.

"You never learn, you silly bugger," the red-haired man laughed, eyes flashing. Polished boots planted wide apart in the straw bedding, he was stocky with wide set shoulders, muscles rippling under tight riding breeches, biceps straining at his black frockcoat. The white silk shirt and neck stock appeared almost an affectation in contrast to his weather worn face, flesh tanned by the wind and eyes crow-footed from staring out over the land. Wild red hair hung over eyes which held emerald fire, twinkling now in pleasure, but when he was angry the sparks became an inferno, capable of rooting the object of his distaste to the floor. He had a sense of will and purpose about him, and men stepped aside for him before they realised they had given ground. He carried the strength of his personality like an aura; a man who knew what he wanted and how to get it. He could handle most men with ease, subjecting his will on them without patronising or showing condescension. Somehow, he managed to make it appear a man was doing him a favour rather than obeying orders. Animals too, fell under his spell.

He led the mare from the loose box, then she stood quietly while he flung a saddle onto her broad back. He caught the trailing girth and began to buckle it, then roared with laughter when the mare inhaled. Elbowing her in the ribs, he hauled the girth tighter by another two notches as her breath rushed out. Satisfied it was tight, he patted her.

"You want some fresh air, Blackie? It's a fine evening." The outer stable door opened as he started toward it. A groom stepped inside, carrying a lantern.

"Ah, Mr John. I thought I heard something."

"I'm surprised you can hear anything with those hounds talking." The groom glanced at the open door. Howls and barks rose into the night from the kennels.

"Last feed they had was a dead sheep yesterday, sir," the groom remarked. "They're hungry now. You should have a good day's sport tomorrow, sir."

"So shall you. Tom'll be riding as Huntsman and I'd like you as Whipper-in. That all right with you?"

"Yes sir, of course," the groom grinned, thinking of his bonus as well as the day's sport, plus the pleasure of authority over the local gentry, however brief.

Richard John slapped his shoulder. "Good man. How's Blagdon Driver running?"

"Fit as a pup, sir. Best nose on him in the pack." He followed as his master walked the black mare to the mounting block. When Richard John swung into the saddle the groom touched his forelock with a "Good evening, sir," then crunched away across the gravel to the servants' quarters above the stable block.

The saddle creaked, the mare pawing the drive. One leather was short. Richard slipped a boot from the stirrup and adjusted it. Better. He sucked the cool night air down into his lungs. Funny how he rarely got that feeling anymore. Apprehension, fear, whatever it was that crawled in your bowel. But there was something there. He just couldn't put a finger on it. He was glad though. An edge made it more worthwhile somehow. He glanced across at his home, well lit, outlined in the darkness. Cliff House was huge and sprawling, whitewashed, with chimneys on nearly every corner where rooms had been built on, each with its own cluster of windows, curtained now. The main drawing room looked out over Saltburn Glen, the canopy of trees like a lumpy green carpet below, an extension to the sloping lawn. To the rear of the house was a paddock, knee deep in rich meadow grass, then beyond the boundary fence yellow fields newly shorn of winter feed reached toward Skelton woods.

It was a country gentleman's house, and he remembered how proud he had been the day he bought it. But the thrill of acquisition had long withered and the years had turned it into his home, ownership now an accepted fact. He wondered then at how quickly his sense of achievement had faded, almost as if his success was only reflected in the eyes of other men. They saw material wealth and notoriety, but he had long since realised success was merely a state of mind, and then only fleeting. What really mattered was knowing how short one had fallen of original goals and one's self imposed standards. It was not what you did, but the way you did it, and most of all, doing it well. Aware of those shortcomings, the success that others envied seemed shallow and too easily won.

But what satisfied him now? In his youth he had been grateful for a straw mattress, a bowl of oatmeal porridge and a crust smeared with beef dripping to fill his belly. Now, even the softest feather bed, roast pheasant and the finest French Burgundy did little to satisfy him. It seemed the simple pleasures were indeed best. A good horse, the wind in his hair, and most of all a good woman, sleepy and warm with him in bed. It seemed the edge of danger was almost more necessary now, like citrus fruit to rejuvenate his jaded palate. The thrill of testing his wits, especially against the law, and the risk of being caught.

Why else would he be riding on a night like this?

He shrugged away depression, laughing aloud at his introspection. Blackie trembled beneath him. "Come on, you old bugger!" he roared, rowelling her flanks. The mare laid her ears back, stretching into a full gallop, hooves scattering gravel from the drive. At the gateway he turned her head toward the beach beyond the steep gradient of Saltburn Bank. Although he knew he was risking both his neck and hers, he let her run.

His face creased in a wild grin. If the Good Lord wouldn't take Richard John then the Devil could.

*   *   *

A horse snickered, igniting Ronald Hardiman's growing anger. "For God's sake keep that animal quiet," he muttered from between clenched teeth. The culprit made an apologetic face and placed a hand over the horse's muzzle. Couldn't blame the animal, really, Hardiman told himself. After waiting three hours, the aroma of meadow grass up here on the west cliff must have been making the horse's stomach grumble with hunger. His twelve Dragoons were bored and hungry too. So was he, but then he was used to waiting. It came with the job. Six years a King's Riding Officer, he had wasted many such nights, waiting for cargoes that never arrived. Only this time the informer had sworn his information was genuine, not like other times when he had spent all night waiting only to go home shivering in the dawn. Often, the next day he discovered it had all happened five miles down the coast in the opposite direction.

Tonight would make up for those times. He would derive great pleasure from riding into the smugglers with his twelve Dragoons. The soldiers were all Irish, from the 6th Enniskillings garrisoned at York. They had volunteered for waterguard duty to add an extra two pence a day to their weekly wage of seven shillings, and also freedom from the stifling discipline of the barracks. They only discovered the harsh reality of their posting when they were billeted on the coast. The locals despised them, the intermarried fishing communities laughing openly when the Dragoons clumped up and down the narrow streets in their heavy leather boots. With tricorn hats and scarlet jackets with white cross-belts, they stood out from the fisher folk like royalty from peasants. One local girl had succumbed to the charm and twinkling blue eyes of an Irish trooper, but had made the mistake of telling her brothers. The next day the Dragoon had been found barely alive, his once handsome face battered to pulp.

What made the job hard were standing orders not to use violence, except in self defence. And there was no defence for laughter and derision. The beaten trooper was unable to identify his assailants and it was impossible to prove the girl's brothers were responsible. Since then the troopers had kept well away from local girls, no matter how enticing.

Hardiman sympathised with them, and suspected if the opportunity arose tonight, there would be more than a few broken heads among the smugglers. Although just as conspicuous himself in the villages on his beat, dressed in a black frock coat and breeches, mounted on a black stallion, at the end of the day he could go home to his wife and forget for a few hours. While he played with his children, the Dragoons were frightened half the time of being poisoned in their billets.

But he had his own complaints too. In six years as Riding Officer, his salary had never increased, £90 a year. The incentive, of course, was prize money. He was entitled to half the resale value of whatever he confiscated, the remaining half claimed by the crown, but even then he often had to wait many months for settlement. It all called for careful accounting and spadefuls of patience.

His beat extended from Teesmouth to Staithes, some fifteen miles. If he had learned anything since his transfer to North Yorkshire, it was that every villager in Redcar, Marske, Saltburn,

Skinnengrave and Staithes was a rogue. If they had arms to carry and legs to walk, they were either active smugglers or in league with a gang in some form or other. Even those holier than thou men of the cloth, the clergy, were not exempt. If they didn't openly encourage the trade, then they did not refuse when offered a dram of hard liquor on housecalls. Even women with suckling babies had been known to hide kegs under their skirts.

A Riding Officer could trust nobody. At least with his new detail of a sergeant and eleven Dragoons, even if they were dumb Irishmen from the bogs, he had a little help in his one man war against the whole population of the coast. Before the Dragoons' arrival the situation had deteriorated so badly he had been forced to give ground. After confronting a gang one bleak dawn on Redcar beach, they had fled, abandoning almost a thousand gallons of gin. The next day a brick had been hurled through the window of his cottage at Marske. The attached note declared if he didn't stay at home the following night and sleep in his own bed, then he wouldn't sleep anywhere, ever again. And neither would his wife and children. Personal threats he was used to, and accepted, but his family had never been threatened before. After deliberation, he had complied with the note's demands. Keeping his family secure indoors, he had been first to cross the doorstep the next morning. At the bottom of his vegetable garden in the privy had been a half anker of brandy, a small bag of precious tea and some paper wrapped tobacco, obviously torn hastily from a bale.

Other notes had followed. Perhaps a suggestion that a ride to Redcar would be tiring and that he would be better occupied watching Marske beach, where of course he spent a fruitless night. But after that first time, the other bribes were easier to accept. Also, he slept more soundly, knowing he had protected his family. He knew who was responsible, if indirectly, for the notes and the payoffs left in the privy; Richard John of Cliff House at Saltburn. In his two years at Marske, Hardiman had met that name in almost every investigation. Before Mr John had moved up to Cliff House he had been the landlord of the Ship Inn on Saltburn's foreshore. Hardiman had gone through his predecessor's numerous reports and had lost count of the times the Ship Inn had been searched. Not once had anything incriminating been found. More infuriating was that Richard John seemed to delight in the raids, smiling and overly courteous.

Now, it appeared Mr John had grown too presumptuous. Somewhere he had offended someone who had too much influence to be ignored. And that someone had blown the whistle. A heavy handed letter had reached Hardiman from the area comptroller, attached to a copy of a letter from the comptroller-general in Southampton. The contents had been precise. An example was needed, and Richard John had been chosen. He must be apprehended, preferably red-handed, but he must be caught.

Which was why Hardiman was standing in a damp field on the west cliff above Saltburn at midnight staring out at the black North Sea, acting on information provided by an informer. It was also why twelve restless Irish Dragoons were at his back, all eager to ride, and a king's cutter *Ferret* was riding to anchor off Marske, some three miles away, ready to aid Hardiman should a lugger put into Saltburn Bay.

"'Scuse me, sor," the Irish sergeant said.

Hardiman lowered the telescope and rubbed a weary hand across his eyes. He grunted a reply.

"Would it be all right to allow the men to eat now, sor?"

"Very well," Hardiman agreed, thinking how Navy captains always sent ship's hands down to breakfast when action seemed imminent. The king liked his men to fight on full stomachs. As the troopers began to rummage in their saddlebags before the horses were led away to graze, Hardiman compressed his spyglass and untied the bulky handkerchief his wife had pushed into his pocket. There was bread and cheese, but he chose the apple for its juice. After a cursory rub along his breeches, he took a bite, absently watching the night while he ate. He had almost reached the core when he saw it.

"Sergeant! Mark those flashes!" He pointed out to sea.

The NCO was beside him in an instant. They both counted. Three. Neither man spoke. The light sparked again. One, two, three. Hardiman held his breath. The informer had said three answered by three, then four answered by two. There was no possibility of seeing the replies from land, the lantern would be shielded . . . Four. There it was.

"How many, Sergeant?"

"Three, then four, sor."

"Agreed. Right, send me Fowler, he's the fastest rider." He fed the apple core to his horse, wiped his hand on his thigh then began to scan the night with his telescope again.

"Sir?"

Hardiman gave a ghost of a smile as he looked the soldier up and down. "Fowler. At the bottom of Marske High Street there'll be a boat manned by Customs men. They're waiting for you. The message is POSITIVE SIGHTING. REQUEST IMMEDIATE ASSISTANCE. Got that?"

"Yes, to be sure, sir. Positive sighting. Request immediate assistance."

"Right, then ride straight back here. Now get going." Hardiman listened to the drumming hooves die away in the night. The rest of the men were watching him, some still holding pieces of bread. He gestured for them to finish then turned back to look over the bay.

He allowed himself the luxury of a smile. Well, Mr Richard John, your time has come.

*　　*　　*

Richard John swung down from the black mare, breathing heavily, exhilarated by the headlong ride down Saltburn Bank. The night breeze had rekindled his enthusiasm for the task in hand and he cast a professional eye round the Ship Inn yard, full of harnessed ponies, each carrying empty panniers. Most wore nosebags, crunching on top quality oats to give them stamina and wind for the long trek inland to the villages where willing hands would unload them. He nodded at one of the men tending the animals, then pushed open the back door into the inn. Low ceilinged with heavy timber beams and a cool flagstone floor, the bar was packed with drinking men in seaboots, the air fogged by tobacco smoke. Every eye turned toward him. He strode through the drinkers, his self confidence almost a visible aura that exuded power.

"Tucker?"

A lanky man, with a hatchet face, wearing a fishing guernsey, was already rising from his seat.

"All set?"

"Yes, sir. The signal's been seen." Tucker took out his watch and prised open the lid with a dirty thumbnail. "Five after midnight. Should be ready for us in half an hour. I've told these lads who were on lookout to lend a hand on t'beach."

"Which lads?" As Richard John tapped his thigh with a riding crop his coat opened slightly to reveal the butt of a pistol sticking from his waistband.

Tucker spoke hastily. "Val here and his mates."

Richard John's eyes flickered to the youth. "You're Jackie Rudd's boy, aren't you? Val? A strange name for a lad."

Those green eyes were penetrating and Valentine had to push his shaking hands behind his back. Nerves made his voice a croak. It was the first time Mr John had spoken to him directly. "My name's Valentine, sir. I was born on 14th February."

"Ah, yes." He seemed a likely looking youth. His green eyes flashed back to Tucker. "I'm relying on you. Stay with it. I have some business to attend to."

*   *   *

On the foreshore, the sea breeze ruffled Valentine Rudd's hair, his nostrils full of the tang of salt and seaweed. Behind him hooves rattled on stone in the yard as the pannier ponies were organised into strings of ten. Ahead, seaboots crunched on shingle before the boatmen reached the sands. Here and there hurricane lanterns glowed. When Roland and Tommy joined him, he started down the beach, eyes beginning to adjust to the night. It was half tide. Waves steadily encroaching up the shore had already reached the dozen boats, tethered to stakes driven into the sand shortly after nightfall. They hadn't yet begun to tug at their painters and Valentine admired somebody's accurate guess. He could see there wasn't enough seawater underneath to lift the keels of the clinker-built cobles, but they would not need carrying far. Figures were stooping over the boats, making sure oars and other gear was handy. A man turned and beckoned.

"You! Come here. Oh, it's you, Val. Well, lend a hand to float her off. We could use you at an oar too." He paused, dropping his head to peer at the dark water swirling round his seaboots. "As well as t'tide flowing, I think she's starting to come away. It'll be hard pulling tonight."

As he bent to grab the coble's gunwale Valentine glanced ahead at the sea. If he wasn't mistaken... yes, he could see her now, a different pattern of shadows in the darkness. He squinted, concentrating. Yes, her lines were exactly as he remembered. *Morgan Butler*, edged in so far her keel must be scraping along the seabed.

"Come on, heave."

Valentine switched his attention back to the coble. Together, he and the four men lifted and began to splash out. Valentine felt his arms almost being pulled out of their sockets as he strained. Walking became more difficult as the sea swirled up over his ankles to climb his calves, soft sand underwater sucking at his boots.

"She's off." Magically, the weight of the coble disappeared. Valentine climbed in and found a thwart amidships to sit down, lessening the rocking as the others came over. The last man gave her another heave seaward then expertly scrambled aboard. Standing in the stern he hung the rudder on its pins before knocking on the tiller bar. Valentine lifted his oar and dropped its thole onto the pin, holding steady until everyone was ready.

"Right," said the steersman. "All pull."

The four oarsmen bent their backs and dipped blades. The double-ender began to make way, bows rising to the incoming waves. Facing backward, the rowers could not see their destination, only the now dark inn and the other dying lights from the cottages. The lanterns might be out, Valentine knew, but nobody was asleep. With the men all on the beach, the women waited anxiously behind closed shutters.

Valentine's chest muscles were tearing, then they were beyond the breakers. The work eased, the coble gliding over dark water, the swell their only enemy. "Nearly there," consoled the steersman. Valentine stole a glance over his shoulder. *Morgan Butler's* tall masts loomed up into the sky, timbers groaning as she lazily rolled. Rigging humming, she was hove-to into the breeze, facing Marske in the west, and they were closing on her port side. The steersman was holding over the tiller, ready to lay alongside.

"Port side, ship oars," the steersman advised.

Valentine heaved his dripping blade inboard, the coble beginning to rock in the swell as she lost way. There was a dull thump and the journey was over.

"Heave a line," a voice called softly from the lugger.

They secured fore and aft. Valentine and two of the men clambered over *Morgan Butler's* gunwales. She was flush decked and about fifty feet long, Valentine estimated from what he could see. Her hatch covers were off and already a double tiered stack of kegs stood next to the nearest hatch coaming. Crew lined the rails, hands resting casually on the barrels of swivel guns. With a start Valentine realised one was aimed at him. He shuddered inwardly. A more villainous bunch he had never seen. Somebody nudged him.

"They say he's a right evil sod, her captain," Roland Flounder whispered. "I saw him once with Mr John."

"You'd best shut up," Valentine admonished. "They might be listening. Who're you with?"

"Me Dad. We're tethered for'ard of you ..."

"Start working," a voice growled from the shadows. Captain Josiah Brown appeared, hands on pistol butts.

"It's him," Roland muttered, vanishing like a wraith into the darkness.

Valentine met the captain's eye for a second, then to his surprise, Josiah Brown winked. Valentine choked off a laugh of relief and stepped to the tier of kegs.

He was soon sweating.

*   *   *

The woods were dark as the gate to Hades. Ronald Hardiman cursed under his breath as he led his horse through the stunted trees to where Skelton Beck snaked along the bottom of Saltburn Glen. Nervous, the Dragoons trailing behind stumbled, rustling leaves and snapping twigs while horses rattled bits, saddle leathers creaking. Hardiman was glad he had ordered no weapons should be loaded. One of them would probably have tripped and discharged a pistol. Occasionally he could hear a terse order from the sergeant to keep strict silence.

Everything had gone to plan. Trooper Fowler had delivered the message to *Ferret*, and ridden straight back. After waiting half an hour for the king's cutter to get under way, Hardiman decided to move his men into position. Muffling the animals' harness, they had begun the tricky descent. He could only hope the surf on the beach was drowning any noise they were making.

After what seemed an eternity the ground levelled off. He waited until they were all down, then began to lead off toward the shore, following the stream bed. Up on the top of the Brotton side of the glen he could see the lights of Richard John's property, Cliff House. The building was enormous, like a squire's, and all bought from contraband profits. Basically an honest man, Hardiman lived in a rented cottage, with little likelihood of ever owning his own home. He shook his anger away. Best to keep clear of emotion when executing his duty.

But as he turned he caught the flicker of movement in a window of the big house. Curiosity drew his gaze back. He cursed himself for a fool, hoping the distant figure, obviously a woman, was Richard John's daughter. Three times he had seen her, and each of those times was carved into his memory. The first time the beat of his heart had almost been crushed to silence by her beauty. Pale skin as smooth as a peach, her figure was ripe like a woman's, but carried with a lust-awakening innocence, seemingly unaware of the havoc she caused when men looked at her. Her finely drawn features were framed by a soft cloud of blonde hair, and her eyes were unforgettable, a startling blue, clear and fresh, unjaded by the world. Although Richard John's wife was a beautiful woman, there was no contest between mother and daughter. The daughter's innocence added to her appeal. To strip that naivety away from her would be a pleasure worth having. As he stared, the curtain closed, and he banished the imagined image of her naked from his mind. There was other business to be done.

He looked off to the mouth of the glen, beyond which lay the sea. To the right, on the other side of Skelton Beck was a field housing lime kilns next to a farmhouse and barns, below the road which curled up the edge of Huntcliff toward Brotton. Directly ahead loomed Cat Nab dominating a row of cottages in its lee.

Hardiman gestured for a halt then beckoned the sergeant forward. "Take three men, cross the beck and that field there, then set a trap on the road. I'll get round the edge of Cat Nab, so when the cutter gets here we'll be in position to block all the escape paths." He studied the NCO's face. He had given him the fewest men, knowing the sergeant's experience would be worth another three men. "Any questions?"

"Sor. You just want me to sit tight?"

"Yes, but don't forget to cover Little Dale which runs off at a tangent just behind the Ship Inn." He grimaced. "We're going to be spread thinly, but there's no alternative. We just have to do the best we can."

"Where will you be, sor?"

Hardiman waved a hand toward the bulk of Cat Nab. "I'll take the rest of the men to the left of the Nab, then I'll leave three there to cover the beach. When the cutter arrives I'm going to make a charge with the other five troopers on horseback into the smugglers to confuse them. That should drive some into your hands and the others along the beach this way. All clear?"

"Yes indeed, sor."

"Carry on then."

The Irish sergeant saluted then turned away, whispering to his men. With little fuss, three troopers separated from the line then eased their horses down into the beck to wade slowly across the knee deep water. Hardiman watched them go then waved the others on.

"And keep it quiet back there!" he rasped.

*　　　*　　　*

Lieutenant-Commander James Major peered up at his filling sails as slapping feet walked back down the deck. The anchor was catted and *Ferret* was crabbing in her usual style before the sails were properly trimmed and she gained steerage way. He was crowding all sail to dash down into Saltburn Bay. There was no way of knowing how much time he had before the smuggling lugger spotted him. Major grimaced. If his opponent was Josiah Brown then there was all possibility of a bitter fight. Major knew Brown of old, their meetings always inconclusive. Tonight he hoped to change all that.

When *Ferret* had been ordered from Newcastle Upon Tyne down to Teesmouth, it had seemed likely there was a purge in the offing. The Tees estuary was the route inland to the large merchant ports of Stockton and Yarm. However, after a week of beating back and forth across the river mouth, making random searches of incoming shipping, they had made few confiscations, and Lieutenant-Commander Major had wondered if he'd read the signs wrongly.

But on the eighth day *Ferret's* mate, Jack Dykes, had answered a signal from Tod Point, a peninsular sticking out into the estuary. When Major had crawled out of his bunk and dressed, the cutter's boat had already put ashore and was fighting back through the cross currents. When Riding Officer Hardiman boarded *Ferret* after his ride on the choppy river, his face was blanched, but half a tumbler of confiscated brandy brought colour to his cheeks. After offering a letter of identification, he stressed the importance of apprehending Richard John.

It all began to make sense. Before leaving Newcastle, Major's superior had told him to offer all assistance possible to Riding Officers should his aid be required. Richard John and Josiah Brown. The two names brought a scowl to Major's face. They were fast becoming living legends along the Yorkshire coast, their exploits making Customs and Excise look foolish, and that made James Major extremely angry. His was an honourable profession. Poorly paid, yes, but he was working directly for the king, collecting the crown's dues. There was nothing amusing about that. Well, well, Richard John and Josiah Brown. *Ferret's* commander had begun to smile, especially when Officer

Hardiman disclosed he had reliable information a run would occur at Saltburn the following night.

It was time for a little legend killing. Not only would there be a substantial amount of prize money, but the kudos attached to the capture of such notorious offenders could not fail to impress their respective superiors...

"Weather that helm, hard away!"

James Major smiled as the mate snapped out a string of orders. *Ferret* had righted onto her course now, fore and aft sails eating their fill of the breeze. A bow wave cleaved under her forefoot as she clawed off the shore. To starboard the few lights from Marske were falling astern, replaced by the silhouette of St Germain's church on the headland. Beyond stretched an unbroken line of tall sand hills merging into a low clay cliff which lined the beach all the way to Saltburn Bay.

Ferret breasted the surf and started rolling and pitching among the bigger swells. Her bowsprit gored the oily sea, showering the foc's'le. Aft on the quarterdeck, Major enjoyed the cold salt spray, a hand touching the rail as she crested then plunged into the next shallow trough.

"She's coming away, sir," Jack Dykes commented on the growing sea.

Major smiled. "She is too, Mr Mate. Have the four-pounders loaded, ready to run out. The swivels too. And clear for action." It was an order Major always felt faintly ridiculous giving aboard the tiny *Ferret*. She was nothing more than a captured smuggler herself, bought from a prizemaster by the crown and refitted. A thief set to catch a thief, despatched to protect the king's subjects from their own dishonesty and thievery...

"A light, a light..."

"Whereaway?" the mate demanded of the lookout.

"On the starboard quarter. Under the cliff."

James Major's face set hard, a tendon writhing in his cheek. He nodded to the mate. "Very well. Silence the lookout and get him down from there. I want you to get some sail off her so she comes up nice and quiet. Then have the men stand-to." He turned away as Dykes issued the orders. When the mate looked expectantly to him again, Major continued coldly, "I'm going to round to seaward to block *Morgan Butler's* escape. I'll be standing by the stern swivel on the lee side. When we close, I shall hail him in accordance with the regulations. If he refuses to give himself up, I shall warn him of the consequences. If he still refuses..." Major's lips creased into a mirthless smile. "...then, Mr Dykes, we shall have a fight on our hands."

As sail was shortened, *Ferret's* bow wave collapsed and she glided silently through the night toward the great black shadow of Huntcliff. The cutter's crew remained mute, only her timbers creaked and groaned as the breeze sang softly in her rigging. As they closed, the glass revealed a flotilla of small boats jockeying over the waves to and fro from the lugger which was lying hove-to, her head to the wind.

Major knew it was only a matter of time before *Ferret* was seen. He was relying on them being too busy to notice his approach. He waited at his loaded swivel, the lanyard brushing the back of his hand. Nerves began to crawl restlessly in his stomach. *Morgan Butler* was growing bigger by the second. He could discern her size as her masts emerged from the night, carrying sail, ready to run. He counted two fishing cobles alongside and eight plying toward the beach ...

"Ahoy there! Stand off!" a voice shouted.

Major saw men freeze on the lugger's deck, each carrying a keg. He was closer than he'd hoped. *Ferret* sailed on.

"Ahoy there! I said stand off!" The voice was angry.

Major lifted his speaking trumpet. "This is His Majesty's cutter *Ferret*! I order you to stand search. I will send a boarding party!"

"Like hell you will! Sheer off I say!"

"If you do not submit, I shall be forced to fire into you!"

Major warned. There was no answer. He only had to wait a few seconds and then he had complied with the regulations. His hand felt for the swivel gun lanyard and wrapped it round his fingers, ready.

Then there was an orange flash as one of *Morgan Butler's* guns fired. As the sound shattered the night, shot howled through the rigging a yard above *Ferret's* quarterdeck.

With a scream James Major jerked the lanyard and his swivel gun crashed, flinging a hail of canister shot.

THREE

Ferret was masked by smoke. Her five starboard four-pounders fired as they came to bear, long tongues of flame licking at the night. Shot the size of a man's fist pummelled *Morgan Butler*. She flinched under the onslaught as rigging parted aloft. A heavy topyard plummeted down in a ravel of ropes and pulleys. It crashed onto the quarterdeck, furled canvas knocking the helmsman from his feet. Captain Josiah Brown, close by, grabbed an axe. After chopping away the debris, he pulled the man free then turned back to glare across the water. The flashes from *Ferret's* broadside seemed to have burned their image onto his retinas, his night vision destroyed. He cursed, mind racing. How much longer to unload the rest of his cargo? What was the Excise cutter's armament, and how many men did she carry? Could *Morgan Butler's* crew hold them off until the remainder of the cargo was transferred to the boats...

"Fire the swivels! Pick your target!" he bellowed. Now he understood why they hadn't seen her approach. She had stolen up bows on, and was only now rounding to starboard, blocking the route to the open sea. The guns crashed, spewing nails and musket balls toward the Exciseman. More suitable for close work, they inflicted little damage. "Mate!" Josiah Brown shouted. "Is the cargo done yet?"

"For the best part, Cap'n." The mate appeared from the smoke, eyes swinging back along the deck to assess the situation. "The men who aren't at the guns are throwing out kegs as fast as they can. But the boats are slow coming alongside... Look at that, will you?"

Captain Brown tore his eyes from the Exciseman and followed the mate's arm. Pinpricks of light were flashing on the shore, and now he could hear gunshots and shouting. "Muskets and pistols. The damned Dragoons are in on it too." He swung back. *Ferret* was hauling her wind, closing. He began to sift alternatives. The king's cutter didn't dare over-reach toward Huntcliff and come under Butler's stern to rake because the hidden shelf of rocks would chew into the cutter's keel and catch her aground. She could either come about to run down again or... *Ferret's* four-pounders thundered out another broadside, blotting out his thoughts. Shot screamed over their heads, punching holes in the spanker sail. One ball ploughed into the gunwale, tearing up splinters of white wood that scythed across the deck. There was an agonised scream.

Or he can board us now...

"He's closing fast, Cap'n."

Brown made his decision. "Get oars and spars ready to fend off so he can't grapple, then trim the sails and cut the anchor cable so we can run."

"What about the boats?"

"They'll have to take their chances. Jump to it."

"Aye aye." The mate strode for'ard, shouting for men to grab anything to help fend off. "Stand by to repel boarders!" Near the main hatch Roland Flounder was sagging at the knees under a half-anker of brandy. His hair was plastered to his face and his shirt was dark with sweat, muscles screaming. He had been transferring kegs from the holds to the boats. Now he was confused. Another vessel coming out of the night, cannons firing at them. As the mate passed, he straightened up, but the mate shook his head irritably. "Not you. Keep unloading."

Roland paused, staring over the starboard gunwale. He could see *Ferret* gliding in, guns blazing. It was almost as if he was watching it all happen to somebody else. He remained completely detached as the cutter loomed large, men swarming across her deck brandishing cutlasses and boarding pikes.

"You! I said carry on!"

Roland blinked, focusing on the angry mate who was stalking back along the deck. He nodded, turning his back, then hefted his keg to the port rail. Knees hard against the bulwark, he leaned out, but there were no hands to relieve him of his load. Cursing, he leaned out farther. The coble had gone, vanished into the night, the fishermen pulling hard for the beach. As he saw the splash of oars twenty feet away, Roland started to curse. Then there was a crash and the weight of the keg threw him flying. With arms and legs windmilling, he plunged into the cold dark water.

Within seconds he was drowning.

*   *   *

Valentine Rudd was up to his thighs in the surf. Stooping over the rocking coble he hoisted a brandy keg onto his shoulder. As he took the weight the sand underfoot reached up to suck greedily at his ankles. He turned away and began to wade toward the ponies who were fetlock deep in the sea. Led in pairs down to the water for loading, they would be taken back up the beach to be roped into a string for the trek inland. Valentine had almost reached them when a deafening explosion split the night behind him. He swung to look at the sea.

The shadow of another vessel was nearing *Morgan Butler*. Then came the flash of orange and the crash of a swivel gun from aboard the newcomer. It was quickly chased by five overlapping thunderclaps from cannon. Valentine stared at the drifting grey smoke, fascinated. As the cannon fire died away, yells and screams swung him round to face the beach again.

Men were running. The ponies, skittish now, backed in circles, seeking hard sand for a footing, manes tossing as they dragged their handlers out of the water. Boats were beaching on either side, men leaping out and splashing through the shallows. A pistol cracked, the muzzle flash over on the right. A scream, then the pounding of hooves.

"In the King's name!" a voice shouted. "Stand still! You're all under arrest!"

"The damned Excise," a voice cursed.

Valentine pivoted on one foot, the weight of the keg rendering him stiff and awkward. He saw Tucker emerging from the darkness, away from a beached coble, seawater foaming white about his boots as he strode ashore. He was pulling a pistol from his belt, teeth glittering white in the shadows of his long face.

"Load the pony, lad," Tucker muttered. "Take no mind of the Exciseman, then get them up the beach. I'll take care of that damned king's man." He moved on past, grim faced, left arm waving like an officer on a battlefield. "Stand with me! They'll not take our cargo!"

As Valentine moved toward the ponies, he saw other fishermen creep from the night, a few with pistols but most with cutlasses and daggers. He moved to steady a pony with his free hand so he could lower the keg into a saddle pannier. The handler had lost control. Wall-eyed, teeth snapping, the ponies backed off, fighting the halter.

"Hold them still, man," Valentine growled.

Then they came out of the night. A thunder of galloping hooves. Hoarse cries. Huge dappled grey chargers, necks stretched, ears back and nostrils flared, long powerful legs with heavy steel-shod hooves. Riding low over flying manes were Irish Dragoons, hangars drawn and straight-armed forward like sabres. Crossbelts hung ghostly white across their scarlet tunics as they charged, hardware and saddle harness jangling and creaking. They were the most awe inspiring sight Valentine had ever witnessed. Fast and dangerous, a complete contrast from when the Dragoons plodded dourly round the streets on patrol, wisecracking at each other from the corners of their mouths.

Ahead of the charging skirmish line galloped a black stallion, mouth foam-flecked, white eyed and highly strung. Its rider was dressed in black from head to foot, boots gleaming as his spurs rowelled the black's flanks. He bawled a meaningless battlecry as he raced down the beach, a cutlass twirling about his head.

Bucking and rearing, the pannier ponies wrestled free to canter into the night, their handler running helplessly in their tracks. Valentine stood frozen, keg still on his shoulder as he stared at the charging Dragoons. He could not decide whether to wait, follow the ponies and run for it, or join Tucker's small group of resistance. But he had no weapon.

The decision was made for him. The leader, who he recognised as the local Exciseman from Marske, saw Tucker's forming rabble and turned the black's head. The stallion veered. In his slipstream the troopers swung in a precision arc, line abreast. Bravely, Tucker's men stood their ground, then at the last moment scattered, twisting to fire upward or swing cutlasses at the riders. The black stallion plunged through them, the Exciseman hanging out low from his saddle, blade slashing back and forth. The Dragoons were among them then. Each Irishman of the 6th Enniskillings automatically reverted to the horse drills which had been practised until perfect. Hangars hacked down to the right, then performed an uppercut before swinging across the charger's withers to the blind side and down, then another uppercut, then the backhand slash down and up then back across the saddle and down to the right as the horses kicked and reared on tight reins.

With a start Valentine realised the Exciseman had ploughed straight through and was turning to ride him down. Still ankle deep in the swirling sea, he could see no escape. Already the black's hooves were throwing up spray as they left the sand, the stallion seeming taller every second. The Exciseman wrenched on the reins so the horse's haunches went down, forelegs stiff, frozen in flight, then it reared from the water, hooves churning the air.

Instinctively, Valentine hefted the keg aloft to shield his head. The black loomed above him, the whole sky full of angry, lethal horse, determined to trample him. Valentine's nostrils were full of rank animal smell now. Head down, his hands jarred as hooves battered at the keg, striking sparks from the metal hoops. Then the stallion came down onto four legs, quivering, the Exciseman sawing at its mouth. The horse swung sideways to allow his master a clear cutting field with his cutlass.

Valentine saw the gleam of steel. His own mouth was a silent scream as he pivoted on his heels, bunching his whole weight, the keg rising above his head. The cutlass blade touched his arm then skinned the front of his chest as he strained up onto his toes. With every ounce of strength he could muster, he hurled the keg.

Emotions intensified by adrenaline and fear, he saw every detail of the following seconds. The stallion, head arched toward him, baulked from the flying keg. Hooves scrabbled in all directions, seeking firm ground. The horse plunging and the momentum of the cutlass slash left the Exciseman half out of the saddle. One boot slipped from the stirrup, and with one hand gripping the reins he had only his sword hand to deflect the flying keg. His hand swung up. The half-anker smashed into him, dashing the blade from his hand. Eyes impossibly wide, he was driven from the saddle. Legs kicking, he somersaulted backwards over the black's rump to sprawl in the sea.

Before the Exciseman hit the water, Valentine sprang forward. He slapped the horse's flank to run it off then groped in the black sea for the fallen cutlass. Hand tight about the hilt, he lunged forward. Two steps and he was there.

The Exciseman tried to rise. Breath sawed in his lungs as he fought the weight of his sodden clothes. Spluttering and coughing, he struggled to his knees. Then Valentine was on him.

There was no fear now as he kneed and kicked. The Exciseman shouted, flung on his back once more. Valentine was astride him, pinning him to the sand. A wave broke, washing over them, the cold sea draining their strength. Valentine's eye caught the gleam of a weapon in Hardiman's belt. With the cutlass in his left hand, he lunged with his right. He wrenched the pistol free then awkwardly cocked it. When the hammer clicked back, held against the spring, he pressed it into the Exciseman's throat.

Hardiman's eyes widened in terror as Valentine jerked the trigger. It misfired, dead. Relief sobbed in the Exciseman's throat. He stared at the shining wet face above him, committing every detail of the long face, lantern jaw and straggly brown hair to memory. It was all hard and clear, death, fear and excitement mirrored in the youth's eyes as he flung away the useless pistol.

Hardiman croaked, his voice dredged from the depths of fear. "So you want to make it murder? Smuggling's bad enough, but you'll hang for murder. They'll hunt you to the ends of the earth for killing a King's Officer."

Valentine didn't bother to watch where the pistol fell. Wet powder rendered it useless, so it held no further interest. Instead, he transferred the cutlass to his right hand, then swung it back to begin a throat cutting slash.

The Exciseman gasped. "THINK! Not murder, for God's sake. You'll hang!"

As Valentine's arm flexed to execute the coup de grace, he knew the officer was right. There would be nowhere to hide, and when they caught him, if he lived long enough they'd drag him to the scaffold at York Castle and hang him. He shuddered, shaking with anger and fear, and the numbing cold of the sea. And they quartered murderers after they were dead, flesh stuck on pikes and exhibited on the battlements. He had a sudden vision of the sack being put over his head, hands bound fast, then the rope chafing his neck and the long drop. Even worse, his mother watching, wringing her hands and crying.

The stream of flickering images stilled his arm. As he faltered, he looked down into the Exciseman's eyes and saw the spark of triumph there. His sword arm sagged downward, the cutlass blade dipping into the sea. Almost in a dream, he pushed himself to his feet, then he was staggering away.

After a few paces he paused to look back. The Exciseman was prising himself up onto one elbow, hair dripping, face a mixture of relief and victory. His hoarse croak carried across the swirling water.

"But I know you now, boy. I won't forget this!"

Valentine's mood snapped. Grim, he turned and splashed back to the man he had nearly killed. With a snarl, he swung back his arm. At the last moment during the downswing he twisted his wrist so the cutlass hilt crashed into the side of the hated face.

The king's officer flopped lifelessly on his back in the lapping sea.

*　　*　　*

Roland burst through the swell. Spluttering, he kicked desperately to stay afloat. His eyes cleared and through a hole in the cloud above was a sprinkling of stars. He was grinning and laughing, arms swirling, feet treading water. The roaring in his ears faded, drained away with the seawater. It was then he heard the battle. He twisted in the water. *Morgan Butler* lay twenty feet away, towering above him, sails luffing. On deck men were firing and reloading as fast as possible. Muzzle flashes flung sparks out across the sea, shot howling away to starboard as powder smoke rolled back across the deck and down onto dark water. Roland could not see the Excise cutter, his view blocked by the fighting lugger, but he knew it must be closing from seaward.

Suddenly, his teeth chattered. Exhilaration at being alive was fast being sucked away by the freezing sea. His fascination with the battle withered, the urge to flee growing stronger each second. He twisted away, shoreward, gauging the distance to the beach. Then he saw they were fighting there too. Tiring fast, he knew he would have little strength to join the fray if he ever crawled out of the surf. That left only Huntcliff. There was a notch called Penny Hole where a mooring post stood. Fishing cobles sometimes used the Hole when the weather and tide were too severe to risk running straight in to the beach. It was his only choice.

Something smashed into the back of his head. He ducked away, a wave swamping his open mouth. He came up spluttering, twisting. It nudged him again, more gently this time. He paddled frantically to keep afloat. Then he almost laughed. It was the brandy keg. Even full, it bobbed in the swell. He caught hold of the raised lip round the lid to find it supported his weight. Quickly his other hand grabbed the rolling keg, stabilising it to make a lifebuoy.

He hung on, breath hissing in and out of his lungs with relief, his head above the rolling swell. Panting, he glanced over his shoulder at the battle still raging between the two vessels, cannon fire erupting in the night, the bellowing of angry men carrying over the sea. Then he began to kick, arms resting on the keg, striking out for Penny Hole, hidden somewhere at the base of the black wall of Huntcliff.

He knew it would be a long swim.

*　　*　　*

Alchemy had converted Valentine Rudd's feet to lead. He plodded up the beach, unconsciously circling away from the Irish Dragoons battling with Tucker's band of villagers. Breath sobbed in his chest, a wracking pain that stretched from his shoulder across his ribs. Wet, exhausted and confused, he knew he had to reach the Ship Inn. Then, somehow everything would be all right. Head down, shoulders sagging, he mechanically placed one foot in front of the other. Off the sand now, shingle crunched under his boots. His knees were beginning to shake. Scowling, he concentrated but his body's reaction to the fight with the Exciseman was uncontrollable. Embarrassed, he tried to ignore it, instead squinting ahead, isolating the silhouette of the inn, dark now, squat and solid at the edge of the beach.

The ground levelled off and he angled across to lean against the side wall for a moment, chest heaving. He could not wait too long. His eyes were aching and once or twice darkness blurred the edges of his vision. He shook his head and staggered to the rear of the inn. The yard was empty, pannier ponies swallowed by the night. At the back door he pummelled the agreed signal. The door opened and a hand pulled him inside.

"Give me that," a voice urged.

Valentine squinted and by the light of a shielded lantern recognised Will Chapel, the landlord, reaching open hands toward him. "What?" he mumbled.

Chapel reached up to take the brandy keg balanced on Valentine's shoulder and placed it on the floor. Valentine frowned. He had no recollection of picking it up from the beach.

"And what's that?" Chapel asked, taking the cutlass from him and inspecting it. Valentine became aware Richard John was standing behind the landlord. "Jesus, it's a king's officer's cutlass," Chapel said, handing it to Richard John. "Where did you get it?"

Valentine shrugged. "He tried to ride me down."

"Was it him that wounded you?"

Valentine looked into Richard John's green eyes, then down at his own shirt. Torn cotton hung open, revealing a gash across his ribcage. Blood had saturated the material. Valentine grimaced. He felt no pain, only numbness.

"You've done well, lad," Richard John said, then switched his attention to Will Chapel. "They need me out there."

Chapel shook his head vigorously. "I've sent to Skelton for men. If that Exciseman sees your face, you've had it. He's been warned off, and God knows he's been bribed enough times. His men charge the beach while a cutter attacks the *Morgan Butler* at the same time. It's too well organised. There's something afoot. It's not just the cargo, it must be you they want. You've got to stay out of it."

"But damn it, my men trust me," John said bitterly, trying to push past.

The landlord used a shoulder to block the passage. "You'll be no use to your men in York jail, and that's where you'll be if the Excise see you," Chapel reasoned. "So the run went bad. If the *Butler* gets away, Captain Brown knows what to do. There'll be other days. None of your men will split on you. They know what'll happen if they do. They need the work. No, you've got to keep out of it. And as soon as the king's men get organised you can bet they'll be in here, turning the place upside down. They know there's liquor already ashore." He spared a glance for Valentine sagging against the wall, blood dripping on the flagstones. "And he needs doctoring."

The whites of Richard John's eyes were bright in the dim lantern light. He had already reached the same conclusion as Chapel, but he needed a moment to think. There was something afoot. This time, they really were out to get him. But wanting to – and actually catching him – were two different things. Quickly, he measured Valentine's strength; he was failing fast. They had to move now.

"Come on, lad, follow me." He touched Valentine's arm and shot a glance at Chapel who nodded, turning to lead the way to the cellar down worn stone steps. Lantern-light was reflected off rough hewn whitewashed walls. He squeezed between ale barrels until he reached a solid wall of casks, each laying on its side, tops facing outward. He swung a fist at the lid of the bottom one. The wood gave with a click, and the top swung outward. It was false, one foot and a half deep, actually a little cask on its own, with a tap so ale could be drawn off on inspection. Behind lay a dark hole.

Richard John took the lantern, stooped and disappeared through the opening. Squinting, vision hazy, Valentine felt Chapel's hand on his back forcing him to bend low then he was literally pushed through the opening. The cask lid closed behind him. Through the shell of the cask, the wood staves echoing beneath his boot heels, he followed the light into a tunnel. Able to stand upright, he placed a steadying hand on the damp clay wall.

"Where...?"

Richard John glanced back as he walked. "Branches run into the cliff for stow-holes, but the main passage runs up to Cliff House. Not far, but it's a steady climb."

Valentine doggedly placed one foot in front of the other, hand scraping the wall. Totally exhausted, the slash across his chest had begun to throb. Absurdly, he wondered at the mammoth task of cutting the tunnel. He'd heard talk of it, used when no ponies were available to move the contraband inland. On those nights, all the kegs disappeared into the Ship Inn, but he suspected few men had actually seen the tunnel. On the left, the dark maw of a branch beckoned. Valentine peered in, but could see nothing. He stumbled then, slipping down onto one knee. His hand pressed down on the floor, then something furry scurried over his fingers, squeaking. Valentine reeled away, grunting with shock. Ahead, Richard John stopped, swinging so the lantern shone its feeble flame back down the passage.

"Only a few rats, lad. Nothing to worry about."

Valentine was still on his knees. He couldn't be sure whether the darkness closing in was that of the tunnel or in his mind. Everything was blurred round the edges, and it didn't seem to matter if he was standing up or on his knees. He couldn't lift his head. Forcing himself, he looked up as lantern light shone down over his face. For a moment he thought he saw Richard John staring down, then everything disappeared as darkness claimed him.

*   *   *

Tommy Tiplady was leading two loaded ponies across the sands up from the waterline when *Morgan Butler* opened fire on *Ferret*. Startled, he faced the black sea, eyes wide as the king's guns retaliated, gouts of flame erupting into the night. The ponies began to wrench at their halters, eager to flee from the deafening gunfire. As he concentrated on preventing their escape, Tommy heard a bloodcurdling cry further down the beach, accompanied by the rumble of galloping hooves. When the Irish Dragoons thundered out of the night, they swept by some fifty yards below him, almost at the breaker line. He began to run.

Skidding and sliding, Tommy stumbled, half-dragged by the pannier ponies. Ears back and wild eyed, they plunged up the beach through the shingle to escape discharging muskets, the clash of steel, and ship's cannon bellowing over the dark sea. The yard behind the Ship Inn was bedlam. Men and ponies were scattering in all directions. Feet on hard ground, Tommy managed to halt the headlong flight of his own two charges. Someone shouted he was to break for Saltburn Gill and make his way to the Duke William Inn at Skelton.

His heart hammered in panic. Frantically, he cast about for a familiar face to fall in with. Impossibly, he recognised nobody. Inky pools of darkness and half shadows masked faces moving between milling animals. Breathless with fear, he abandoned the search. He turned, running between the two ponies, guiding them toward the lane that curled up Huntcliff. At Brotton, two miles inland, he could turn west toward the rendezvous at Skelton.

The ruts in the lane did nothing to slow the ponies. Kegs bouncing, they tried to canter while Tommy fought for control. As they climbed, the gunfire diminished, his panic easing as they moved into the enveloping silence of the night. The ponies responded too, the stubborn tattoo of their hoof beats on the coach road shambling into the regular rhythm of a trot. Heads nodding, blowing through dilated nostrils, they chewed less at the bit, jerking only a little at his almost dislocated shoulders.

Unconsciously, he began to mouth a prayer, ragged breathing settling. He patted the pony's neck on his right. His hand came away smeared with lather. Yes, I was frightened too, he admitted, uttering a soft laugh of relief...

"Hold!" a voice called from the darkness. The tone meant business. "Who goes there?! In the King's name! Stand and be searched!"

Tommy froze, squinting ahead to scour the shadows. Silhouettes rose from either side of the road, a white crossbelt almost luminous, a glint of a blued barrel with fixed bayonet rising to cover him. His first thought was that his hands were full and he was helpless. Instinct took over. He recalled the knife stuck in his belt. He groped blindly for the hilt, drew it clear then began to hack at the rope holding the kegs across the back of the pony on his right.

"I said HOLD! Come forward and be recognised!"

Tommy hissed through clenched teeth. Snap, damn it. The blade sawed at the hemp. For God's sake, snap. He glanced up. The figures were moving toward him. Cursing, he attacked the rope. It gave a little. He was trembling. The pony also sensed the menace from the night. It began to shift from hoof to hoof, haunches swaying. Tommy sneaked another look. One soldier was approaching from the hillside on the left, another from the right, emerging from the roadside hedge. Only about ten feet away now. Break! Eight feet now. The pale ovals of their faces were beginning to show features.

The rope gave. The keg on the far side bounced on the road, spinning away at an angle. The soldier there cursed, jumping away from the careering cask. Tommy caught the nearest keg, fumbling, a hand hampered by the two bridles. He hefted the keg, ready to throw. The closing Dragoon read his mind. He side-stepped. The keg flew past his head. With a grunt of satisfaction, he lowered his musket to use the bayonet.

Tommy squeezed against pony flesh as the fourteen inch steel lunged at his stomach. The tip snagged his coat, then the Dragoon's face came close. Tommy's arm swung up in a punch. Knife still clenched in his hand, his knuckles were like rock. His fist crashed into the Irishman's head. The three-cornered hat spun away as the soldier crumpled.

"Stand still or I fire!" a voice commanded from the night. Tommy grabbed a handful of mane and swung up onto the unloaded pony. Knees gripping fat ribs, he heeled the animal savagely, wrenching its head toward a little used path that led to the top of Huntcliff. He jerked the bridle of the laden pony, dragging it into a canter in his wake.

A Dragoon opened fire. A musket ball screamed past Tommy's head. He hugged the pony's neck, mane whipping his face as he slapped the reins to urge more speed as the path twisted upward.

Voices were shouting below. "Stop him!" He heard the commanding voice bellow. "You! Get the horses! At the double!"

Then he could hear the thunder of hoof beats and the crashing of the chargers as they rode hell for leather up the path after him.

FOUR

Freshening wind caught Tommy's hair as he emerged onto the rim of Huntcliff, the pony stumbling beneath him. He was out of musket range. Gasping from tension he reined in, the two ponies blowing hard. The long climb up the poacher's path had taken them almost two hundred feet above the snaking coach road. It was almost black as pitch on the cliff, darkness that provided shelter and succour, but also served to breed fear of the unseen and hide the unknown.

As his breathing slowed he could hear the dragoons calling to each other as they galloped up the path, grain fed chargers making short work of the climb. If he rode a straight line following the farm tracks to Brotton they would easily overhaul him. The pannier ponies were well suited for long journeys at a walk, but not racing through the night.

He leaned forward, peering left and right, seeking escape. There had to be some way to evade the troopers. The night provided no clues, then he twisted to squint back down the path. A light! They had a lantern! He cursed. If he left the path they would be able to follow. The ground was damp underfoot, good for tracking, not wet enough to lose them in a mish-mash of cattle tracks. He cursed again. The light was growing nearer, dancing up the hillside.

He kicked the pony into a canter. There was a way. And he would be able to save the two half ankers of geneva too. Tugging at the lead rope of the second pony, he urged his mount along the cliff-top path. He knew the Dragoons would be frightened of plunging over the edge in the dark. And any time they sacrificed could only benefit him. After half a mile the track swung toward Brough House running by a fence tangled with briars. That was the place.

Turning as he rode, Tommy saw the lantern light appear on the cliff-top, then begin to trail him. They were like hounds. Well, he would fox them, and good. He started to smile. The track curved ahead and he eased the ponies down to a walk, pulling over to the left. He dismounted onto grass without leaving boot heel marks in the well worn path, then wrapped the reins round a fence pole. He untied the girth rope of the second pony, then hoisted the kegs from the animal and carefully lowered them to the ground. He unwound the reins then slapped the flanks of both animals. Startled, they plunged away along the track into the night.

Tommy grinned. It just might work. He dumped the two kegs in the shadow of the briar hedge some yards from the path. But when he turned to look back the lantern was rapidly approaching. One of the Irishmen must know the path, he thought. Annoyed, he dropped to hands and knees and squirmed as far under the briar as the thorns would allow. His chin pressed to the grass and the two half ankers of geneva for company, he watched the light bobbing toward him. As the troopers neared, his heart hammered and he was sure his breathing was deafening. There seemed no way to avoid detection.

Plodding hoofbeats grew louder, along with the creaking of harness. There were two. One held the lantern low while the other leaned over the neck of his horse to scan the trail.

"I'm not knowing why we're going so slow," the lantern carrier grumbled. "I'm sure I was hearing those ponies galloping a few minutes back. If you're asking me, he's to hell and gone."

The second man grunted, loath to take his concentration from the ground ahead. "You might be right and you might be wrong," he muttered grudgingly. "Only these hoof marks'll give us the truth of it."

Tommy held his breath, chest pounding. They were level now, moving at walking pace. The two chargers were still blowing after galloping up the cliff path, snorting and dipping their heads, chewing on steel. When he could smell warm horseflesh, Tommy hugged the earth, face down, fearful the whites of his eyes would betray him.

"Bejesus, be getting on with you," the lantern carrier said irritably, urging his horse forward.

"Yes, yes," the other mumbled, voice fading as they followed the spoor. The tracker snorted. "Here. They started running here." He kicked his horse into a trot, suddenly eager. "Come on with you, then. You're wanting to catch him so badly."

Then they were gone. Tommy saw the lantern dancing away from him as they followed the path curving toward Brotton. He sighed with relief. Safe. Now he could make for Brough House and hide the contraband in a barn for later collection. Mr John would certainly be pleased with him. Evading the Excise and saving two of the kegs. The pannier ponies, running free, would eventually quieten down, graze for a time then find their way home.

He crawled from his hiding place then hoisted the rope up onto his left shoulder, one keg against his chest, the other nudging his back. They were heavy, the rope cutting a furrow through his thin coat. He grimaced. Sure he could bear it. Over the fence and a short walk. If worse came to worst he could cut the rope, carry one to the barn and come back for the other. Time to be moving before the Dragoons discovered their error and came nosing back to sniff him out.

The briar tangle was too thick to attempt so he ranged along the fence until he came to a clear stretch. Chest high with three bars. Here would do. Carefully he gripped the top rail and stepped up onto the low bar. The little barrels were awkward. They swung wildly after only the barest body movement, the rope gnawing at his shoulder blade. Steady. The rear one thumped into his backbone. He grunted then eased a leg over the top rail, moving slowly so the kegs remained stable.

His foot touched the centre bar on the other side. With a crack the rotten rail splintered and parted. His leg dropped away, the top rail biting into his groin. He groaned as his body jerked over, falling to the right. The keg against his chest swung sideways like a pendulum past his right shoulder. Caught by the top rail for an instant, it snagged then toppled back over behind him. As he fell forward, behind him both kegs slipped down the other side of the fence. The rope across his neck became a hangman's noose. Yanked up short, one leg was twisted uselessly beneath him, broken, the other caught in a tangle with the splintered rail.

"J-J-J-J-Jesus," Tommy croaked. Both hands grabbed the tightening noose to tear it free. His good leg jerked, scrabbling to gain a foothold to ease the pressure. It would not work. The bar had somehow speared through his trousers and was jammed into the ground.

Then he began to appreciate the true weight of the half ankers. They hung motionless, a perfect counterbalance using the top rail as a fulcrum, his own body suspended by the neck. He strained, fingers ripping at the rough hemp. It was useless. The noose continued to tighten.

Eyes wide to the moonless night, he felt as though a blade of tempered steel was driving through his windpipe, slicing up into his skull. Lungs screaming for air, he began to pray, the words in his mind a fearful speeding scrabble of half finished sentences. Asking forgiveness, making excuses, offering promises, begging release, pleading for mercy, hoping for a bargain ...

The knife! Sobbing, he released the rope from his right hand, choking, squirming as the noose jerked him upward. He groped frantically at his belt. It had been there before. Where ...? Gagging with anguish, he grabbed the rope again, remembering.

He must have dropped it on the road when the Dragoons halted him. He had cut the pony's rope with it. Suddenly, it seemed important to recall the incident clearly. Oh, the pain. The rope burned like fire. He resisted its pull with all his strength. His brain was going to explode.

Then nothing mattered anymore. Tommy Tiplady's eyes bulged as screaming nerves pushed them out of his head, his swollen tongue purple as death thrust it from his mouth. The half ankers hauled him upright, jamming his head against the top rail, staring blindly into the night. The kegs had done their work well. But then, they held the best. Top quality geneva. Guaranteed.

*   *   *

The axe descended in a clean arc. Strands curled away from the wound in the thick hemp cable stretched across the block. The mate hacked again. The anchor cable parted, the severed end roaring out through the hawsehole to disappear with a splash into the sea. Immediately, *Morgan Butler's* head swung off the wind, bowsprit pointing to the open sea. The mate grinned, turning to shout, but the crash of swivels swamped his voice. The king's cutter was still firing too, broadsides thundering across the narrow reach of water.

On the quarterdeck Captain Brown scowled as shot smashed through the lugger's frail planking. Glancing aloft, he hoped there was enough rigging left to manoeuvre. *Morgan Butler* heeled beneath his feet and he started bawling orders. *Ferret* was running down under a sudden squall from seaward toward Huntcliff. She was too close to weather Saltburn Scar which would already be reaching out to snare her keel. Her only choice was to swing starboard toward the beach which would bring her ploughing past *Morgan Butler's* stern.

"Avast heaving there!" Brown shouted to the line at the main braces. When the helmsman turned with a look of concern, Brown growled, "Hold her, damn you."

"Aye aye, Cap'n."

Brown fingered the transom swivels, coolly checking their loads and firing mechanisms. He could not allow *Ferret* to come too close because she would rake, but he wanted to strike another blow before he ran. The two guns were set, charged with canister for maximum effect at short range. He turned a weather eye on his sails. Anchor cable cut and canvas on her, *Morgan Butler* was in irons, the wind driving her slowly backward, the swell starting to cream under her transom by the rudder. He glanced at *Ferret* running down fast, bowsprit swinging east, her main gundeck battery silent as her men reloaded. He measured the sea and the wind carefully for a few moments. "Let her run!" he shouted.

The helmsman spun the wheel. Her rudder caught the flowing tide and she began to pay off, head swinging seaward. When her stern faced the beach, the sails were hauled round, men stamping at the braces as canvas boomed above. Unleashed, *Morgan Butler* began to run, bows smashing through the incoming swell as she bucked over the waves. To starboard, barely yards away, *Ferret* was heeling under the pressure of rudder and sails to avoid running onto the beach.

Captain Brown grimaced as *Morgan Butler* danced on the oily sea, then grinned when he saw the Customs' cutter was heeled so far over, her broadside was aimed at the sky. The grin turned to a chuckle as he yanked the swivel lanyards one after the other. Great holes appeared in *Ferret's* straining canvas, blocks and halyards falling from aloft to trail overboard as she careered on toward the tide line.

Brown watched her struggle. It was brief revenge for the king's men interrupting his night's work. Reverie broken as *Morgan Butler* heaved again beneath his feet, he heard his men cheering. He stifled his grin and growled.

"Silence there! Mr Mate? Lay aft. I want parties organised. This vessel may be under way, but she's by no means shipshape..."

*   *   *

"He's shaking with cold, poor lad."

The concerned matronly voice invaded Valentine Rudd's head, competing against his chattering teeth. He lay with eyelids squeezed closed, pain rumbling like thunder in his temples. A hand touched his shoulder and he flinched, shrinking back towards the protection of unconsciousness.

"We can't leave him down here. He'll catch his death," another voice commented. "He needs to be warm, tucked up in bed."

"But Mr John said nothing about bringing him into the house," the matron advised.

"It doesn't matter. I'll answer to him..." She faltered. "...I think he's waking."

Valentine's eyelids felt glued together. He forced them apart then snapped them shut when his iris' reacted to the lantern one of the women held. He tried again, more slowly, opening them to slits into which light poured in a blur. His vision focused until he could see the woman bending over him. About the same age as his mother, the lantern glowed through her blonde hair, making a halo about her head. Although weak, suddenly he felt safe in the warmth of her smile, almost as if she brought the sun down into that cold dark place. He held her gaze for some seconds, divining her concern for him, then when she looked away he followed her gaze to an older woman, apparently a maid.

"Come on, Mabel," she said, "Let's get him upstairs."

"But Mr John..." the maid protested.

"I'll answer to my husband," the lady with the halo snapped, turning her smile onto Valentine again. "Come on, help me."

He winced as they lifted him, pain skewering his ribcage, an abrupt reminder of the cutlass blow. He stood with head hunched, chin digging into the blanket they had wrapped around him. Now he could discern beyond the small circle of lantern light. He was in a cellar; stone steps rose close by. Contraband casks, bales of silk and tobacco were stacked against one wall and in the other was a dark opening. He remembered then. The tunnel. Soft clay walls. Dark and damp. Searing pain and dizziness. But worst of all, the rats... Involuntarily, his knees sagged.

"Come on. Valentine, isn't it?" the lady with the halo asked. He nodded and allowed the two women to flank him as he began to painfully climb the steps. At the top a trapdoor lay flung back to admit a shaft of daylight. He emerged into a loose horse-box, his feet shuffling in straw bedding. Leaning against the wooden partition, chest heaving, he watched Mabel lower the trapdoor with its flush fitting ringbolt, then carefully disguise it with straw. She saw him watching and grinned.

"What the Exciseman don't see, his heart don't grieve, eh?"

He liked her then. She was one of them, conspirators all, free-traders, against law and the king. She took his arm and they led him into the passage. Most of the stalls were occupied. Horses stamped and stretched inquiring muzzles, snorting and shaking out manes. When they reached the outer door Mabel peered outside.

"Nobody about."

He hobbled into the yard, boot-heels scraping on the cobbles. It was cold and grey, the hour after dawn. He shivered and the angel wrapped her arm about his shoulders as they walked toward the main dwelling. Even in pain, Valentine looked at the building with scarcely concealed interest. Cliff House oozed an aroma of wealth, solid and secure on the lip of the glen. Valentine realised there was almost no smell of the sea, only the dampness of morning dew on the grass, the air still and sweet. Nearby in a hedgerow, a lark began to sing, its lone voice pure and vibrant as it called across the countryside. The best hour of the day; the tranquillity and serenity made Valentine's heart ache.

"In here, Valentine." At the kitchen door, he looked back over his shoulder. Even the stable block was nearly as large as a whole row of cottages, roomy enough to stable twenty horses and two or three carriages, yet still provide living quarters for grooms and drivers.

Inside the main house's kitchen a log fire was burning at the range, warmth reaching across the flagstone floor. A blackened pot full of boiling water hung by a hook over the flames. Overhead, pots and pans were regimented in neat rows above a scrubbed pine table, a dresser displaying plates behind. The hearth boasted a rag rug and on either side stood oak ladder-back chairs. In the corner a sink as big as a horse trough had its own pump. The kitchen, Valentine thought, was more luxurious and twice the size of the entire ground floor of his mother's cottage, where his whole family lived and ate and spent the evenings round the fire.

"Sit him down," the angel said as Mabel fussed. Valentine sank gratefully into a chair but the fire was too hot after the damp chill of the cellar. His face was burning, the flames hypnotic. Ready to fall into sleep's healing embrace, he roused himself as hands eased the blanket aside and opened his shirt. He heard them gasp when they saw his sword wound for the first time. The maid fetched a pair of scissors and began to chop away his shirt.

Valentine stirred with panic. "No, my mother..."

The angel scowled. "It's ruined anyway. Don't fret, I'll give you another."

Her voice reassured him and he turned tired eyes on her gentle face. But when her hands lifted the hot dripping cloth to swab the gash his teeth snapped together. The pain was a stabbing red hot poker. His vision blurred and then darkness came crowding in.

He crawled back to consciousness three hours later. Aware of the noise first, the bustle of a busy kitchen, he opened his eyes. Mabel was at the table, pouring brandy into silver cups. Behind her, a scullery maid was chopping vegetables, but close by, watching over the simmering contents of a pan was another girl. Ignorant of his gaze, she continued to work, and he watched expressions chase each other across her face in rhythm with her thoughts. After some time he realised with a start he had been so absorbed he had been holding his breath. It rushed out in a sigh and she swivelled to look at him.

Full faced, she had eyes of startling blue, almost unreal like a shallow Caribbean cove in the Windward Isles. Her pupils were like windows to another world, where disruption and violence were deposed by tranquillity. Now, they clouded as she scowled at him. Challenge was written there too, a wildness and anger that made him ashamed she had caught him intruding on her privacy. The sudden explosion of feelings she invoked confused him. He had never experienced anything like it. Insides churning, he was embarrassed, uncomfortable, inadequate. He divined her powerful and independent spirit, and he wanted to reach out and touch her to be sure she was real, to caress her soft skin and bury his face in the freshness of her hair. He wanted to tell her of the emotions she stirred in him, but she seemed cold, disliking him for some unknown reason. Instead, wary, he remained silent, mouth arid.

She looked away. "He's awake now, Mabel."

The maid glanced up. "And about time. The doctor's been and stitched you up. Says you'll be good as new in a few days..." She was interrupted by the yard door being thrust open. Richard John stood on the threshold, dressed in hunting pink with white breeches tucked into gleaming black boots complete with spurs. At his throat was a silk neck stock studded with a diamond pin, his red hair crushed under a riding hat. As usual he was slapping his thigh with a crop.

"Come along with those stirrup cups, Mabel. The pack's getting restless and the followers are thirsty. I want to be out of here in ten minutes. We're going to draw Hagg Whin first and if it's blank we'll move on to Forty Pence Wood."

"Is my brother riding today?" the girl asked from the fireside.

Richard John smiled at her. "Yes, Tom's out as Huntsman. Couldn't keep him away, not if I tied him to his bed. You mark my words. He'll be Master before very much longer and I'll be out of a job." He laughed. "He loves those hounds. He's all ears when they're working a copse, and when they begin to talk he trembles with excitement. When the fox is hallo-ed, he's up in his stirrups and calling to them, then chasing he's shouting 'Hie over, my little darlings' as they jump the fences."

The girl smiled softly. "You love them just as much yourself, Father. Mr Richard John, Master of The Cleveland and Roxby Hunt. You love to blow your hunting horn and direct the followers," she teased.

"Aye, you're right, lass," John softened, "but not to the exclusion of all else. Tom'd do nought but ride to hounds every day and sup every night, yarning about old Reynard's sly tricks." He shook his head, green eyes following Mabel as she carried the silver tray out to the yard where riders and hounds milled restlessly, the sound of stamping hooves and an occasional bark reaching the kitchen.

He snorted, looking at his daughter again before his gaze came to rest on Valentine hunched in the fireside chair. "So, you're back with us, lad. Think you can walk? Missy here'll take you up to a bedroom in the West Wing." He stressed the last two words, glancing at his daughter. She caught the inflection and nodded. "A couple of days and the doctor'll be back to cut the stitches."

He grunted as Mabel came back inside, followed by the

hatchet faced Tucker who looked pale. Richard John eyed him coldly. "I told you not to come here when the hunt's meeting. There's too many people out there who would like to tie your face and mine together."

Tucker shuffled his feet. "You knows I wouldn't have come, Mr John, if'n I didn't have to."

John slapped his thigh with the riding crop. "Well? Spit it out. The day's wasting."

Tucker pursed his lips. "Hardiman searched the Ship Inn this morning. He had smoke coming out of his ears and his face is bruised black all down one side. He's swearing he'll have the culprit hung..."

Richard John glanced quickly at Valentine's dropped jaw then choked off a laugh. "What for? For clouting him one? He deserved it."

Tucker's head jerked, shocked by Richard John's derision. "He said apart from obstructing a King's Officer, it was attempted murder."

"He'll have a hard time proving it. No witnesses, were there? But our young Valentine has ten who'll swear he was at home with his mother all last night." He waved the issue aside. "Anyway, what of the cutter? "

"*Morgan Butler* got clean away, and all but ran the Customs cutter up the beach. She's almost dismasted, moored in the bay with her men trying to organise a jury rig. I don't think she'll be interfering with the rest of the run. That was what I came for. Is it to be transferred to..."

Richard John cut him off. "We'll discuss it later." His green eyes switched to his daughter. "Well, Missy, are you going to get him up to bed or not?"

"Of course, Father." Her eyes of Caribbean blue turned on Valentine again, but their depths were chilling.

Valentine struggled to stand when she slid a hand beneath his armpit. Pain burned through him again, a rake whose red hot prongs furrowed his chest. He teetered, the room spinning. Forcing himself to take long deep breaths to bring the nausea to rein, he produced the faintest of grins. "I'm ready if you are."

"A likely tale," Mabel said, taking his other arm. A woman either side taking his weight, they guided him to the door into the main house. Before they left the kitchen Valentine turned slowly.

"I'd just like to thank you, Mr John, I..."

The riding crop waved irritably. "Think nothing of it, lad. Now get yourself to bed. Tucker here'll let your mother and father know where you are." Richard John turned away to resume his conversation with the smuggler.

After negotiating a corridor they turned right into the West wing to the foot of a staircase. Valentine peered up at the long flight and groaned inwardly. Up on the first landing was an alcove. The centre shelf carried a huge silver rose bowl bursting with blooms. He glanced at the girl next to him and thought, yes, that's what her cheeks are like. Soft as a rose petals. She caught him staring again and made an impatient little sound, urging him to mount the stairs.

He fought pain every step of the way. With the girl beside him and Mabel bringing up the rear they made a grotesque procession, moving one pace at a time. When they reached the landing Valentine was breathing harshly, arrows of pain shooting through his chest.

He looked up at the next flight and shook his head. "I don't think I can go any further."

The girl snorted, then disentangled herself and reached for the rose bowl. After placing it on the floor she turned back to the alcove and fiddled with something, her back obscuring his view. Wooden panelling swung back to reveal a doorway five feet high. He could see a narrow room containing a bed and wash stand, lit by a single window.

"A secret room," he said, frowning. "But surely the window gives it away."

"Nobody would guess from the outside.," she said irritably, turning to the maid. "I'll see him into bed."

Valentine stooped to grope his way into the room. When he reached the bed his knees were sagging. Gratefully, he lowered himself onto the soft mattress, feet still on the floor. He looked up into her eyes. "You know my name. What's yours?"

She eyed him sharply. "Margaret, why?" Then she removed the blanket from his shoulders and produced a long nightshirt. "Get this on then take off your trousers and get under the covers."

"It's a beautiful name, Margaret. It suits you." he said, painfully lifting his arms so she could slip on the soft cotton nightshirt.

She glowered. "Enough talking, get into bed." When he tried to maintain the conversation she shushed him and helped him lay down, then tucked in the crisp sheet. "You rest while I go back down for some soup."

"Was that what you were making when I woke?"

"Yes."

"You made it for me?"

She raised an eyebrow, mocking, her voice scornful. "Not for you. There's kitchen staff to cook for the waifs and strays my father brings home. Lie still and I'll be back soon." With that she turned away.

Alone in the secret room, Valentine revelled in the luxury of the feather bed. His own cot was crude, the sheets well worn, not best cotton like these. He knew now why he hadn't recognised her. He had only ever seen her in the distance, too far away to appreciate her true beauty. He smiled to himself. Margaret. Margaret. He liked the sound of her name. It rolled round his tongue, rich in texture and flavour. It was silly, he knew. He had known several girls called Margaret and yet the name had never sounded so good or enticing before...

When she returned from the kitchen, Margaret walked slowly

so the steaming broth would not spill over onto the tray. She eased into the room which held nothing but the sound of his breathing, deep and even. She placed the soup by the bedside then looked down at him.

He was fast asleep.

FIVE

Hardiman slammed the door of the Ship Inn behind him, drowning the jeers of the fishermen crowded inside. Three Dragoons waiting on the foreshore turned grim faces to him. Scowling, he pushed past to stand alone and look at the sea to soothe his ragged nerves. He would jail Will Chapel the landlord just as surely as he would jail Richard John. Christ, the way they had laughed when he searched the buildings. And if they didn't laugh, they wore that self-satisfied Yorkshire smugness pasted on their ugly faces. And what did he find? Nothing.

After stamping through the cellar, prodding and poking, ears growing redder by the second, back upstairs he had raked the drinkers for a sight of that youth who had attacked him the previous night. They had made jibes about his face too. He knew how bad he looked. A bruise the colour of a black plum covered half his face. Not only that, but the youth had taken his cutlass when he fled. Jesus, another deduction from his salary. The only redeeming factor was that when he eventually found him, as surely he must, he would stamp on him. First would be obstructing a King's Officer in the pursuance of his duty, but even better, the second charge would be attempted murder. And for that he would make sure he was hung, drawn and quartered.

Hardiman glowered. Unfortunately, there was no possibility of that, but perhaps the judge would condemn the youth to ten years in His Britannic Majesty's Navy. Those ships had to be seen to be believed. Rotten, weevily food and slime covered water, no leave for the full stretch and only the women the captain allowed aboard in port, mostly pox ridden hags. The cursed youth would learn the meaning of discipline. Floggings for the slightest misdemeanour were commonplace, and there was always some petty officer eager to have the cat-o-nine-tails let out of the bag to lick some unfortunate wretch's back with its cruel tongues.

Besides, Hardiman would beat the hell out of the youth before he even arrived at court. Nothing that would show, but he would feel pain, and plenty. He would learn not to tangle with the King's Officers. Hardiman cursed then raked up a gob of phlegm and spat onto the shingle.

Ferret was moored in Saltburn Bay, figures moving on deck working to clear debris then rectify damage from the fight last night. As he watched, a boat was swung out and lowered into the waves. It bobbed as the oars dug into the flowing tide, bows pushing toward the beach. Hardiman waited, the Dragoons mumbling behind him. It took five minutes for the jolly boat to cut through the breakers and glide into the shallows. As the keel ploughed into sand, an officer rose from the sternsheets and stepped over into the shallows to splash ashore. Four men jumped over after him, all armed. Hardiman recognised Lt-Commander James Major as he strode up the beach, every inch the captain; tall with a back ramrod straight, chin tilted upward, nose sniffing the air.

He strode to where Hardiman waited on the hard sand above the tide line, then jerked his head tersely in greeting. It was obvious he was as angry as the Riding Officer over their embarrassing defeat the night before. A suit of sails blown to rags along with running and standing rigging shot into an unusable mess of trailing cordage.

"I hope you had more luck than I," Major remarked dryly, turning slightly to gaze at the crippled *Ferret*.

Hardiman's eyebrows crowded down over his dark eyes. "We caught four ponies, each loaded with two half ankers of brandy."

"None of the perpetrators?"

The Exciseman avoided a reply, sucking his teeth in disgust.

It was reply enough for the cutter captain. He speculatively eyed the bruise spread like a birthmark down the other's face. "It wasn't for lack of trying, no doubt. What now?"

Some of the misery evaporated from Hardiman's face. "They haven't finished the run. Knowing John, he'll switch to another pre-arranged entry point. It's up to us to find out where." He raised an eyebrow. "I have a source."

"How reliable?"

"He was right about last night."

Major's eyes strayed to his cutter swinging on her anchor cable as the tide continued to make. "If it happens in the next day or so you'll be on your own, unless another cutter is cruising off the coast. I have a spare suit of sails but the standing rigging needs a lot of work. That lugger's swivel guns were devilish effective at close range. The mast is damaged too. My carpenter advises me if I crowd sail or meet foul weather, it'll snap like matchwood. When the men finish the jury rig, I'll have to put into port while the rest is put to rights."

Hardiman frowned. His task was growing harder by the minute. The Customs cutter had been his ace. He stared out to sea, the sea that brought his troubles but which also provided his salary. After a few moments a hollow cough splintered his concentration. He turned irritably to find the Dragoon sergeant waiting at attention.

"Yes?"

"Excuse me, sor, but we've found one of the smugglers." The Irishman's face betrayed nothing.

"Where have you got him?" At last something's gone right, the Exciseman thought.

"In the yard behind the inn, sor."

"Let's see what he has to say."

"Begging your pardon, sor, but he's dead. We found him on

the cliff top, hanging over a fence... "

"Did one of your men shoot him? I'll have his guts..."

"No, sor. He had been carrying two kegs tied together and somehow he fell and the rope strangled him."

Hardiman's thoughts raced. "Any idea who he is?"

The sergeant pursed his lips, the bearer of bad tidings. "Sor, it was Tommy Tiplady, the informer."

Hardiman turned away toward the sea so the Dragoon and the *Ferret's* captain would not see his face. He closed his eyes, then cursed long and fluently under his breath.

*   *   *

"Get your boots off my desk!" Richard John roared from the doorway of his study. Still dressed in hunting pink, his white breeches and riding boots were spattered with mud. His neck stock had been tugged loose and his jacket sleeve was torn where a tentacle of briar had snagged his arm after Blackie had stumbled into a ditch. It was small ransom. He could have broken his neck. He strode into the room, glowered at his son Tom and moved behind the desk to the decanter tray. He splashed brandy into a snifter then turned enquiringly, but scowled as he saw Tom already had a glass in his hand.

"I see you've helped yourself. And I won't tell you again about those damned boots."

As colour rose dangerously in his father's cheeks, Tom John removed his feet from the desk, slowly, defiantly, his spurs rattling as his heels clumped onto the carpet. He looked much like his father, red haired and green eyed, but where his father's face was lined and set with character, Tom's was weak and open, even naive. He has a tendency to sulk, too, thought Richard John as he looked at his son. How can he look so much like me thirty years ago, and yet be nothing like me?

Tom leaned back in the leather chair, nursing the brandy

glass. He still wore his hunting clothes too. Damned if he ever wears anything else, Richard John mused.

"Well, father?" Tom asked, disinterested.

Richard John's mouth tightened. "It's time to talk business."

Tom winced and made as though to stand up. "Talk about your business, you mean. The one you run with your little band of faithful followers yapping at your heels, and your little secrets like that fisher lad who's been laid upstairs for two weeks, hiding because he almost beheaded a Riding Officer." He shook his head passionately. "I'll have naught to do with the filthy trade. If you want to deal with pirates and have brawls on the beach with the Excise, then you do that. But I'm damned if I will."

Richard John bristled. "It's not just my business, it's yours too. How do you think we can afford to live in this house, but for what you call my 'filthy trade'?" He gestured to the glass in his hand. "You're ready enough to drink the produce. How do you think it got in that decanter but for my 'filthy trade' which, incidentally, also bought your hunters and a ride with the hunt. If it wasn't for all the years of hard work I spent building up my business, then you'd likely be a farm labourer right now and the only bit of you to touch a saddle would be your hands, cleaning it for somebody else's fat arse. It's only because of my 'filthy trade' you're likely to be the hunt's next master."

Tom pushed himself to his feet and planted the glass on the edge of the desk, contents swirling undrunk. "I've heard it all before, father; how it was in the old days; how you and mother worked your fingers to the bone. I'm sick of hearing it. The old days are gone. I can be master of the hunt without any help from you. You can keep your trade and its produce. I want no part of it." He turned to go, candlelight flashing from his spurs.

Richard John's voice was harsh, full of contempt. "You think thirty guineas a year Master's salary will keep you? And what happens when you take a wife? And maybe have bairns? There's more to life than enjoying yourself. Leisure has to be earned, and up to now it's been me that has earned yours. Hunting won't put a crust in your own mouth, never mind if you have a family. Thirty guineas wouldn't pay the servants' wages, never mind the taxes on this house every year. Without my trade, what are you going to do then?" He snorted scornfully.

Tom's glare was a mask of defiance, whether his father spoke sense or not. "I'll manage," he sneered, mouth open as though to say more, but then he turned and stamped out, leaving the door open.

Richard John slumped into his chair, then gulped brandy to drown his anger. He poured more, eyes roving the bookshelf-lined walls of his study, many of them bought because he knew he should read them. But the problem was having the time... So Tom was sick of hearing about the old days? The boy had been given too much too easily. Perhaps to appreciate it properly it had to be earned the hard way, fought for, tooth and nail.

Richard John shook his head. By God, he had learned about everything the hard way. Born the second son of an illiterate tenant farmer in Scotland, he had struggled over his books every evening after days spent on backbreaking chores. His mother, who had received a basic education keeping the daughter of a local squire company as she slaved under a governess, had taken infinite pains to teach young Richard to read and write. And he had hated it. Until the day he had discovered the magic of numbers. Then it all became easy. He had an affinity for numbers and their nuances as some boys have for recognising minute differences in birds' eggs. Columns of figures excited him and fired his imagination. He grasped them easily, at first totalling on paper before he discovered an ability to juggle them mentally. He began to set himself problems, gradually increasing their complexity. He enjoyed it. Numbers were fun. With school education non-compulsory, Richard John had none, the family budget too tight to afford the expense of schoolmaster's fees. Thus, when he reached employable age he had no glowing school report to show a prospective employer, nothing to give any inkling of his potential.

His uncle secured him a job with Laidlaw & MacKay, a stagecoach line operated by a manager for absentee owners. Richard began at the bottom, mucking out the stables in one of their posting houses. His interest in everything was soon noticed and after taking his turn at most manual jobs, within two years he was switched to clerical work. Whenever the line manager visited on his rounds, Richard always suggested ideas. It was simple. He could see it all so clearly. The figures ruled all. Everything else meant nothing. That the columns of numbers represented money was irrelevant to him as no money other than his meagre wage passed through his hands. It was the figures themselves that were important to him. To manipulate and balance them with skill gave him pleasure. That profits were also improved was a secondary consideration personally but of great benefit to his employers.

When the line manager had adopted more of Richard's ideas than he cared to admit, he had installed him at head office. There, his familiarity in working the routes and practical experience gave Richard an edge when implementing refinements. When the manager fell ill Richard did not inform the owners but took on the responsibility of running the line, while the manager still drew his salary to feed his large family. His absence enabled Richard to introduce successively radical improvements. When the half-yearly accounts were audited, the owners were astounded at the increased turnover, cuts in operating costs and the subsequent increased profits. When they confronted the manager now back at his desk, sick leave still a secret, he was unable to provide adequate answers. When young Richard John confidently fielded every question, the stage-line manager realised he could no longer hide his assistant's light under a bushel and quickly heaped praise on him. Within weeks they despatched Richard John southwards to submit a report on an ailing coaching and carting business that was for sale in North Yorkshire.

It was then that figures actually became money for him. When he arrived in Guisborough, examined the books and took an inventory of assets, personally travelling all the routes, he had to admit the line was a good buy, provided it could be bought for the figure he calculated. His Scots' employers decided to acquire the business, but only on condition young Richard would remain in Cleveland to manage it. He agreed. Escaping Scotland's poverty and the ever present threat of enclosures hanging over his family's tenanted farm, his ambitions began to surface. Faced with a wreck of a business, he began from scratch, paring expenses to a minimum, renegotiating mail and carting contracts and improving passenger services. He was also solely responsible for preparing the business' books and accounts.

Hard work enabled him to repeat the process of substantially increasing the owners' profits, this time in Cleveland, but he felt he was due more reward for his labour. Richard had principles. When the owners repeatedly shrugged off his requests for an increase in salary, he took matters into his own hands. If he gained nothing for his employers, he gained nothing for himself but his basic salary. On the other hand, for every guinea profit he generated, he privately credited thirty percent to his own account, his expertise at book-keeping covering his tracks. While the absentee Scots owners were more than pleased at the return on their investment, Richard John's own nest egg grew nearer to hatching.

When covering the line from Guisborough through Skelton and Brotton to the coast, love walked into his life. In Saltburn he met Ann Jameson. Wispy and fragile, daughter of an impoverished squire, from the moment he saw her, Richard John wanted her so badly his breath caught in his throat and his heart hammered inside his ribcage. For the first time in his life he was confronted by a situation he could not handle. From her point of view, Ann Jameson thought the bluff, stocky Scotsman with his fiery red hair and equally fiery temper was fascinating. He was different. Able and competent, he seemed to know exactly where he was going, and there was a vitality and restlessness about him like a blood stallion, eager to be off and running toward the horizon. If he was stiff and awkward with her, then she was all the more pleased. It only proved he was unfamiliar with women.

John's love for Ann also encompassed the place of their meeting. Some months later, the landlord of the Ship Inn at Saltburn confided he wanted to retire to Staithes a few miles along the coast. After scrutinising the inn's accounts, Richard John decided it was time to start working for himself. Careful to ensure he had fully concealed all his tracks in the coach line's business books, John gave notice and used his nest egg to buy the Ship Inn.

To his new occupation as landlord, Richard John brought the creed which had become written on his heart -- Find the right balance. Juggle the figures to give the people what they want at a price they are prepared to pay. He squeezed margins to increase turnover, and with Ann by his side as his wife, they began to provide catering for hunters who came to shoot the gulls along Huntcliff. Visitors and regulars alike were given the best of value and quality until the inn was working at full potential. He had risen to the new challenge of buying and selling in the victuallers' trade and the figures were easy. But Richard John did not like limitations. Dissatisfied, he felt he had merely become a big fish in a tiny pool. A hamlet of poor fishermen and shoe makers was hardly the centre of the world. Outside the limits of Saltburn lay endless possibilities, and he chose to explore them.

In an effort to improve his cellar he approached a brewer in Kirkleatham, a small village five miles to the west. Thomas Earl had learned the art of brewing ale from his father and grandfather before him, but he saw what they had not; that the real money lay in spirits, not beer. All the wealth in the area was spread thinly between the landed gentry, and where those squires might well give their children and servants ale to drink with their meals, hard liquor graced their own tables. And the harder the better. Preferably brandy or gin, sometimes known as geneva. And all spirits carried heavy duties, both Customs and Excise. And the way those squires managed to preserve and increase their wealth was by paying as little tax as possible. A gallon of spirits cost in the region of a guinea, tax another 25 percent. Even the most generous landowner baulked at that.

Richard John saw it differently. He didn't care about the gentry's taxes or greed, only their consumption. A common labourer earning a few shillings for his week's toil could only afford so many tots of gin or brandy. The landowner could obviously afford more, and not only for himself, as he moved in circles where hosts plied their guests with liquor. More consumption. And a man's status was testified by his cellar, so they laid down stock to age and mellow as well as impressing their friends. And then there was the uncertainty of delivery. This was crucial. If they could not be sure of frequent deliveries, then they bought more for fear of lean times. More consumption.

The game became interesting. When Richard John met Thomas Earl, he was immediately aware the brewer possessed two things he badly needed. The first was capital. While Richard John had salted away enough seed money to start a smuggling operation, an alliance with Earl could start them several rungs up the ladder. Enough capital was needed for enough stock to warrant setting up the distribution system John visualised. It was sketched in his mind, highly organised, like the stage line he had run so well.

The second advantage was contacts. As a brewer, Thomas

Earl produced reliable ale for customers which included many of the local landowners. A few discreet words and he would be stocking their liquor cellars too. Reliable service and the message would spread. And with a widening circle of contacts would come influence and power.

It had worked exactly as Richard John had planned. The business expanded on an unprecedented scale, as his secret set of books proved. After first dealing with captains who called in at every bay along the Yorkshire coast to barter with fishermen until their cargo holds were empty of contraband, Richard John negotiated to buy in bulk, so the supply became direct and regular. The captains gave discount as direct delivery negated the need for lengthy trading up the coast, always looking over their shoulders for the Customs & Excise. For two and a half years the business flourished until one lugger failed to deliver. Thomas Earl later discovered their cargo had been sold at Tynemouth where the captain made a greater profit by giving no discount.

Over a hard night's drinking, Richard John and Thomas Earl concluded if there was any squeezing to be done, then they would be the ones doing it. Their efficient distribution network had enabled them to amass enough capital to bypass unreliable contraband runners. They visited the Thames where a prizemaster showed them captured French fishing boats and sloops-of-war sent into port by the navy. More interesting were three luggers, confiscated by the King's Customs cutters. Accompanying John and Earl, captain Josiah Brown showed skills acquired on the route to earning his master mariner's ticket. After careful inspection, he finally selected the sleek and fast *Seawitch*. Unwilling to retain a name already known to Customs and the navy, as soon as the bill of sale was presented, she was promptly renamed *Morgan Butler*.

With Captain Brown reaping high wages, plus bonuses for successful deliveries, the new owners' business again scaled upward. *Morgan Butler* was fully employed, running into ports the length of the Yorkshire and County Durham coasts, Richard John overseeing the whole operation. It all worked so well they even discussed buying another vessel. That was until now...

Lately, Richard John felt something was wrong. At first nothing tangible, just a vague nagging doubt. His customers among the gentry had become wary, reducing their orders, some a touch nervous when he visited their houses. He always knew he would never fully be accepted by them as an equal, no matter how wealthy he became. They clung to the belief the only kind of good money was old money. He accepted that. Anyway, he had little respect for them personally, only their position in society. He had worked hard to earn his money, using both brains and courage. They had merely inherited, and coming into a substantial amount of money was no guarantee one had the brains to administrate it...

It wasn't their attitude that unsettled him, more an uneasiness that fences were starting to close in. Deals started to go wrong. He lost a string of pannier ponies carrying valuable liquor more than once. Then one of his best customers who owned a moorland inn was raided the morning after John's men made a substantial delivery. Soon afterward, a run at Upgang near Whitby was interrupted, albeit unsuccessfully. It was all bits and pieces, but where another man would have dismissed them as to be expected, considering the vast scale of his operations, Richard John found himself adding one detail to another until they became like a jigsaw puzzle, the growing picture almost recognisable. Then the run at Saltburn two weeks ago. Not only the Excise and Dragoons but also a Customs cutter in a highly organised joint attack. It seemed the king's men, once glad to ignore his operations on receipt of anonymous bribes, were suddenly motivated against him. The more he considered it, the surer he was the order had come from high up.

It occurred to him perhaps it was time to retire gracefully. It wasn't as if he had an objective to accomplish any more. Every aspect of running cargoes and distribution was as efficient as possible and he had expanded to the limits that geographical boundaries put on his empire's growth. There was no motive to go on building. He had all the money he needed and financial dealings did not yield the satisfaction they once had. What was the purpose of continuing? Only to hand it over to a son. He sighed. Perhaps he had made a mistake. Earlier, still seeking credibility with the local gentry, he had proposed the forming of the Cleveland & Roxby Hounds. They had agreed, even voting him Master at a nominal salary. His mistake had been to base the hunt at Cliff House.

He had previously lost his two eldest sons to infant deaths, and his one remaining son Tom had taken to the hounds as though born to them. His remarks about Tom loving hunting to the exclusion of all else was an understatement. The only time he was actually alive was in the saddle. When his mud-spattered riding boots were levered from his feet and the hunting horn pried from his hand, he was scarcely a man at all. He had not the barest interest in anything that did not bark or neigh. The allure of women was lost on him. Business meant nothing. Every time Richard John had tried to familiarise him with his various enterprises, Tom's eyes had slowly glazed over. A balance sheet was incomprehensible to him. A margin meant dare he risk his horse at a certain fence; profit was a successful kill; a debit was when he lost one of his favourite hounds, and a credit was congratulations showered after a successful day's riding. His addition was barely adequate to total his weekly expenses and his reading confined to hound-breeding records, his spelling that of a child.

Richard John believed a man was born to be what he would become. He could be moulded a little either way, but the die for his destiny was cast when he breathed his first air of this world. He had tried with Tom, over and over again. No matter what he hoped, his son always rebuffed him, and subsequently disappointed him.

Well, he was damned if he was going to let his empire fall to pieces. If and when he went, either to embrace the grim reaper or to languish behind bars at York Castle, then provision had to be made for his wife Ann, and daughter Margaret. Without a properly initiated heir, it was all a house of cards. Well, if Tom wouldn't replace him as the ace, then he would have to find somebody else.

*   *   *

"You're sure you're fit, lad?" Richard John asked, green eyes sceptical.

Valentine nodded vigorously, unwilling to trust his voice. It was two weeks since he had been injured. Once out of bed the sutures had pulled tightly across his chest. Merely the cutting of them, relieving the pressure, had made him feel strong and healthy again. His recuperation had been spent at Cliff House, and much to Valentine's surprise, Richard John seemed to go out of his way to push him and Margaret together. He could not deny he was flattered – he had thought himself too poor to be allowed to mix with Richard John's daughter – but he suspected perhaps Richard John believed him intelligent enough not to dare becoming too familiar with her. Then again, the older man's smile was too warm, too genuine when he saw them together. The only problem was Margaret. Even though they spent time together, she was cold as ever. Whenever he thought he had made any headway, she would turn those mocking blue eyes on him and he would freeze inside. But he was determined not to give up trying.

And now Richard John had invited him to ride to Hartlepool on business. When the invitation was almost cancelled, John questioning Valentine's ability to ride, an unlikely skill for a fisher lad, Valentine quickly reassured him. He neglected to add he had learned at Richard John's expense, when the village lads had sneaked into Cliff House's paddock and rustled grazing horses for a few hours entertainment. His bareback apprenticeship had served him well.

As they set out along the road to Skelton which would lead to Guisborough then down into the valley of the River Tees, Richard John looked across at his companion. His very youth caused a stab of pain. How the years had gone, endless summers of his boyhood shortened into ever speeding seasons. And the way Valentine sat that horse, as though he had ridden all his life. A natural horseman, his movements were casual, so discreet one wondered whether the horse was taking commands at all. Strangely, he seemed to take no obvious pleasure in his skill, the animal only a means of travel.

"You're not from Saltburn, are you? Richard John asked. "How did you come to be here?" He knew the boy's story but wanted to hear him tell it.

Valentine's eyes flickered. "I was born in Scarborough. My step-mother is from Marske, though, and when my dad married her we came here to live."

"What about your real mother?"

Valentine smiled. "She was called Rose Wilson, my dad's childhood sweetheart. She looked after my grandma when my dad was at sea."

"Fishing?"

"Yes, and one time he got kidnapped by John Paul Jones, the famous pirate. Dad was visiting his sick uncle at Whitby and he went off fishing with his cousin Billy. *Bonhomme Richard*, Paul Jones' man-o-war was off the coast and some of his men captured my dad and Billy then Paul Jones asked them to be pilots for him. They refused and were chained below decks. They were brought up to man the pumps during the battle of Flamborough Head when an English frigate fought Paul Jones, and afterwards dad and the other prisoners had to crew longboats. Any road, they managed to escape in the fog and row home to Scarborough."

"What about Rose Wilson, then?" Richard John prompted.

"Oh, when he got home my dad married her and I was born. Well, not right off. She lost two other babies first. Then there was me, but when she had the next one it killed her. I was still only a toddler, so I never really knew her. About two years after that my dad met my step-mother. Her father, the Rev Beckton, was deputising for Scarborough's vicar for the summer." Valentine laughed. "When dad asked her to marry him, she said she would only live at Marske, so he sold his coble, the *Gin*, and we came over the moors by cart. They couldn't find a cottage in Marske so we ended up in Saltburn."

Richard John knew the story well, probably better than Valentine. He was acutely aware of the standard of living she must have sacrificed to marry a fisherman. She had managed as best she could on little, yet she could be proud of the way she had reared her step-son. "Your step-mother's a good woman," he commented.

Valentine was staring at him. "Yes, she is. She taught me to read and write and how to do the arithmetic. She said once I'd learned, I'd never forget. One of her favourite sayings is that all the knowledge of the world has been written down in books."

"That's true," Richard John laughed. Valentine reminded him so much of himself. Perhaps that was why he liked him. A competence, an aptitude to weigh facts and be decisive, courage when unarmed and on foot to face up to that Exciseman wielding a cutlass on horseback, and then the skill to beat the man and walk away, not thinking of victory, only escape. Intelligent too, in conversation he quickly grasped essential points. The boy was raw material, ripe for manufacturing into an able man.

If only Margaret could grow to like him. He had long worried she was unsuited for the drudgery of marriage to a farmer. He wanted better for her, but knew none of the gentry would allow their sons to court her. So then, what better than if she fell in love with Valentine? He may be poor but there were always opportunities to make money if a man was determined enough. And with the right teacher...

*   *   *

"You stay here with the horses," Richard John said, selecting a sheltered spot in the shadow of some fishermen's cottages. The beach lay stark and flat a hundred yards away, curling in a lazy arc southward into the River Tees some three miles distant. The horses were hidden in a narrow alley between dwellings, yet Valentine could see the whole beach where the run was to take place.

Earlier, they had ridden the ferry across the river from Middlesbrough Farm to Clarence jetty then spurred their horses through the salt marshes in the late afternoon toward the cluster of painted boats and whitewashed dwellings to call on the local smuggling fraternity's leader. Richard John was pleased that Valentine had the sense to remain silent, listening while instructions were given. Offered food, they complimented the fisherman's wife on the plain fare as they ate before nightfall coaxed them to the inn where the fishermen were meeting, ready for business.

Richard John handed Blackie's reins to Valentine. He turned and faced the night where the breakers were crunching onto the sands, then twisted to look at his young companion. "You stay here and keep a sharp eye. This might be an old man talking, but I've had these feelings before and I've been proved right. There's something wrong, and I want you ready to cover my back. You've got your pistol?"

"Yes." Valentine fingered the butt in his waistband. At the cottage he had watched Richard John painstakingly select the most perfect round shot by rolling it across the tabletop when he charged his own pistol, and Valentine had copied him. His experience with firearms was sparse and he was eager to learn anything that could save his life in what was rapidly becoming a hazardous occupation.

"If anything happens, stay well back. Don't charge headlong to help. Wait and see, then make a plan. Brains rule this world – brains backed by power. Never forget that." Richard John stared at him a moment as if to drive his words home.

"What are you expecting?"

The older man pursed his lips. "I don't know. I don't trust these men here. They've never crossed me yet, but that cargo's valuable, and where money's involved an otherwise trustworthy man can turn. When they're all lifelong neighbours, the risk's even higher." He shook his head. "I might be doing them a disservice, but you never can tell. After a while even the dullest of them works out how much profit is involved, and that's when they become dangerous." A rattle of boot heels distracted him. "They must have seen the signal. Remember what I said, lad. Think before you do anything." Dressed in black, his crop still in his hand, Richard John merged into the night.

Alone, Valentine stood between the two horses, patting Blackie's neck as she snickered. A restless wind scoured the beach, flinging sand into the sky. It stung his cheeks and raked gritty fingers through his hair. There was nothing to do but wait. Muffled voices reached him then the scraping of keels as cobles were launched. Squinting, he could see no sign of the lugger offshore. The night swallowed everything.

Minutes dragged. Aware unloading would take a good while, it was useless to give his impatience rein. He caressed the butt of the pistol Richard John had given him. Another present, along with a shirt and dark broadcloth suit, even riding boots that fit comfortably. He felt a little strange in what was to him finery, but he had to admit the change brought confidence.

But waiting was a killer. He would rather have been in old duds, up to his knees in the breaking waves, manhandling kegs from the fishing boats. The bay gelding twisted its neck to nose at his sleeve. He fondled its velvet muzzle, breath warm on his hand. The horses were restless too.

Suddenly Blackie's ears pricked up, her neck stretched toward the alley mouth. It was a full five seconds before Valentine heard them. A low rumble then they came out of the night in a clatter of hooves. Within seconds all was confusion on the beach. Shouts and curses punctuated by musket and pistol shots. Cries of anger and pain. The rasp of steel and neighing horses.

In the alley both horses were wrenching their heads. While he pulled hard on the reins to maintain control, Valentine was ducking under their necks, trying to discover what was happening in the darkness. There was no way to know. He had to get closer. Talking softly to calm the two animals, he backed them down the alley. Behind the cottage he groped until he found a washing line post. He tested it for strength, then tethered the two horses before turning back.

Things were no clearer when he regained his vantage point. Unconsciously, he had pulled the pistol free and put it on half cock. His first instinct was to join the fray, but Richard John's last words stopped him. He did not know who John's men were fighting. He could easily find himself doing battle with his own side. Was it other smugglers or the Excise? He had little doubt that if the smugglers gained the upper hand, Richard John would come to the alley to reassure him. If he did not return soon, then he must have fared badly.

While he stood undecided, unsure whether to follow his impulses, circumstances changed. Abruptly, the battled ceased. Silence remained unbroken on the beach for ten seconds before a curse was snarled, quickly followed by a grunt of pain. A voice bellowed for quiet.

"Shut up or you'll lose your front teeth!"

"In the King's name! Stand fast and be counted!"

Valentine's heart sank. The Excise. Now what? His attention was diverted by a tinder spark. Then a lantern flared, spreading a yellow glow on a circle of faces. Flame was passed from lantern to lantern until he could see Dragoons at the heads of their mounts, pistols and cutlasses levelled at a small knot of fishermen. Figures moved and Valentine squinted, uncertain. Two Excisemen, one tall and well built, black coat open to reveal a pot belly. The other was the King's Officer from Marske. What in God's name did he have to do with this? It was out of his territory.

The tall Exciseman was laughing as he walked around the prisoners. "Hah, Billy Robson and his little brother Davy! Now, there's a surprise." The humour drained from his voice. "You two black-hearted sons of a diseased sow!" He strutted along. "And who do we have here but James Howgego? And such a hardworking honest lad, or so his lying father told me, eh?" He guffawed, then turned to the second Exciseman who was following in his wake. "Are there any faces you recognise, Mr Hardiman?"

The King's man leaned forward, bushy eyebrows low over dark eyes. Valentine almost groaned aloud when he saw Richard John, his clothes making him stand out like a king among paupers. Hardiman picked him without even trying. He pushed through the Dragoons, and even at a distance, Valentine could see the Riding Officer's face clearly in profile. A wicked smile curled his lips, eyes gleaming in the darkness.

"Ah." He thrust his face forward. "Mr Richard John if I'm not mistaken. Gone quiet, have you?"

When John remained silent, Hardiman's anger surfaced. "Go on, deny it, Mr Fancy Richard John with your big house and your pack of fox hounds. So, you refuse to talk. Well, we'll see how much talking you do when I get you into court. Believe me, you'll be standing in that dock the moment the sun comes up. I'm that eager to lock you behind bars..." He laid a hand on the smuggler's shoulder but John shrugged it away. Hardiman snorted. "Well, I've got you now and there's an end to it." He stepped back. "Mr Billington, where's that wagon?"

Another party of Dragoons were gathering a sizeable collection of half ankers of spirits. Dressed in heavy boots and hampered by weapons belts they were making hard work of it, grunting and sweating while the smugglers looked on, faces a mixture of anger and resentment, a trace of fear here and there. When he heard wagon wheels grinding along the sea path, Valentine stepped back into the shadows of the alley. Four draught animals plodded past pulling a box wagon, then the driver cracked his whip. They turned onto the beach and halted. A Dragoon opened both doors at the rear and the smugglers were bundled inside, a bayonet here and there encouraging stragglers. When the doors were shut, a hasp and padlock were slammed in place.

"Sergeant. Keep four men here to clear all the contraband you find," the first Riding Officer ordered. "The wagon'll have to make quite a few trips." He grabbed a half anker of French brandy and hefted it onto the wagon. "Stand guard and make sure it's all delivered to the crown's warehouse." He glanced at the growing pile of kegs. "A pretty penny here in prize money. A good night's work, Sergeant. Carry on."

"Yes sir, Mr Billington." The NCO saluted and turned to bawl instructions at his men while the two Riding Officers climbed aboard the box wagon next to the driver, Billington's boots resting on the brandy keg. Four Dragoons mounted up to ride escort. As the whip lash snaked out over the team labouring to haul the vehicle back onto the road, Valentine watched with a heavy heart, helpless.

*   *   *

Old Stranton brickworks stood on an open stretch of road, pitted sandstone walls facing the sea and the cruel north wind. The buildings sprawled over almost half an acre, most of them dark. One light showed from the soaking shed where the prisoners had been locked up under an armed guard. The other exception was the office where Billington and Hardiman had retired with the half anker of brandy to celebrate their victory.

Valentine crouched in the darkness, holding the half cocked pistol. He had followed the box wagon two miles from the beach on foot, leading both horses. He had no idea why the brickworks had been chosen to house the prisoners for the night, perhaps the jail at Hartlepool was too small. Whatever the reason, he was grateful. The brickworks had not been built as a prison. He had counted the Dragoons carefully and was sure there was only one soldier inside the shed. Once the smugglers had been locked in, the other Dragoons had escorted the wagon back toward the beach. When the wagon did not return after an hour, Valentine concluded the crown warehouse lay in another direction. All the better. He also wondered how many glasses of brandy Hardiman and Billington had quaffed, hopefully enough to make them drunk.

He had waited long enough. Richard John had been right. It was his first lesson. If he had rushed straight onto the beach, he would probably be locked up too. And if his plan, such as it was, went wrong in the next few minutes, then he certainly would be. Either that or dead. He prayed he was not mistaken about the number of Dragoons inside.

He rose to his feet then padded back to the tethered horses. Satisfied they were safely hidden he returned to his vantage point and watched for another few minutes. Nothing changed. Now was the time. He pulled the pistol's hammer back onto full cock and soft-footed across the yard to the office. A guffaw of fat laughter from inside froze him for a moment. Then he inhaled deeply to steady himself. Lower lip clamped between his teeth, he reached forward with his free hand to the door handle.

Slowly, he began to lever it down.

SIX

The door mechanism clicked open. He could hear Billington telling a bawdy story while Hardiman sniggered. Valentine's breathing was rapid, heart beating a tattoo. Sweating, his hair stuck to his forehead. Palms of his hands clammy, mouth parched, his stomach cramped with nerves. He glanced at the pistol and saw he was trembling.

Now. *Now.* With a jerk he flung the door open. Then he was inside, side-stepping so he would not be outlined in the doorway. His pistol was levelled at the open mouthed Excisemen. Glasses in hand, they stared for a long second.

"By God!" Billington roared, red faced, jowls shaking. "What's the meaning of this?"

Silent, Hardiman's eyes narrowed. Face blanched, hatred poured from his gaze in a bitter glacial flow. "You!" he snarled. "Again! Well I'll be damned if you'll get away with it twice. Your card is well marked, boy..."

"Shut up!" Valentine commanded, waving the pistol to demonstrate it covered them both. "Just do as I say. First, give me the keys to the shed."

"And what if we don't?" Billington asked, defiant.

"Then you'll only have one leg to walk on, because I'll blow the knee off the other one," Valentine answered, voice steely.

Billington sat still, paunch overhanging his knees, half empty glass still in his hand. Involuntarily, his eyes wandered to his pistol, removed from his waistband for comfort and laid on a desk. Valentine saw the glance and stepped forward to snatch the weapon. Before either of the officers could move he was back near the door, now with a pistol in either hand.

"Now the keys."

The Excisemen exchanged looks. Valentine could see them totting up alternatives and finally reaching a decision. By now, most of the contraband should be locked in the King's warehouse at Hartlepool. So, if the prisoners escaped, what then? Tomorrow was another day. They knew the culprits and had proof. Only time would be needed to recapture them. The prize money was already safe.

"Get up, slowly, both of you." When they hesitated, Valentine waved his own pistol and carefully cocked Billington's. The hammer catching on its spring was loud. Its menace convinced them.

Billington sniffed disdainfully. "Very well, but you'll regret this..."

"Save the sermon," Valentine muttered, hoping he sounded like a man who would stand no nonsense. "Just walk in front of me, both of you, to the shed and unlock the door." As Hardiman stood up Valentine motioned to the pistol stuck in his belt. "Leave that on the table. Your cutlass too. Carry the lantern instead."

With a glower, the Exciseman complied then stepped slowly to the door. Billington followed, looking back over his shoulder, a bunch of keys jangling in his right hand. Outside, they moved across the yard, Valentine prompting every few steps, the prod of a barrel speeding the pace. They halted at the soaking shed, Billington a little unsteady on his feet, jowls red, mouth slack.

"Open it. You've come to question a prisoner."

Billington sighed. Fingers clumsy with alcohol, he found the right key. The lock opened easily. He slipped off the hasp and used it to pull open the door. Inside, a Dragoon rose from a stool, squinting.

"Who goes there?" he demanded.

"Who do you think, you dolthead," Billington growled.

"We've come to interrogate one of the prisoners."

"Tell him to come forward," Valentine whispered.

"Come here, trooper," Billington muttered wearily.

When the Dragoon came to the doorway, holding his musket at the ready, Valentine stuck a pistol in his face. "Put it down and get against the wall." There was a rustle in the shadows beyond the lantern as the prisoners stirred. The trooper gingerly laid his weapon on the floor then backed away.

"Look out, lad!"

Valentine twisted as Hardiman swung. He fended off the lantern with his left arm then with his right punched the Exciseman on the jaw, the blow weighted by the pistol in his hand. Hardiman staggered. The lantern crashed to the floor, spluttering as oil slopped inside the glass.

"We've got 'em."

A hand righted the guttering light and Valentine saw the smugglers had wasted no time. The Dragoon was pinned to the wall by his own bayonet. Billington was cowering, a burly fisherman snarling down into his face. Someone hauled Hardiman to his feet. It was over. Valentine was trembling, wondering what to do next.

"You did well, lad," said Richard John with a half smile. Taking command, he swung back to face the others. "Tie them up, then be on your way. You know the plan."

"Tie them up? I want me own back," somebody growled, a fist appearing near Billington's face.

Richard John was in no mood for argument. "We're free traders, not murderers. If you kill them, by morning we'll have the whole damned army after us, ready to string us up on the nearest gallows. Do what I say and go about your business." Sure of his authority, he turned away, clapping a hand on Valentine's shoulder. "Come on, lad."

Outside, the night air reeked of the sea. Nostrils cleansed of oil smudges from the lamps, Valentine led the way to the horses.

He was still shaking as he fumbled a foot into the stirrup and swung up into the bay's saddle.

Richard John mounted like a man half his age and tugged Blackie's head round to face the River Tees. He looked back over his shoulder. "Now we ride like you've never ridden before." Spurred, the mare leapt into a gallop. Valentine tucked his pistol safe in his waistband, the other lost in the scuffle. Leaning low over its neck, he urged the bay gelding on. The night became a thing of shifting shadows, wind tearing at his hair and stealing the breath from his lungs, ears numbed by the drumming rhythm of hooves as they raced eastward, following the curve of the shore. White flashes on their left betrayed the waves creaming onto the beach and on their right marsh grass waved spiky silhouettes above the dunes. Fear evaporated, replaced by exhilaration as he became attuned to the animal between his legs, snorting breath loud, flecks of foam blowing back to spatter his face and coat. When the bay side-stepped a half buried log at full gallop, man and horse were so attuned, Valentine barely shifted in the saddle, falling in easily with the resumed gait.

For every moment of that headlong gallop through the night, Richard John led as though following his baying Cleveland Hounds to the kill of a lifetime, the fox of foxes. If he had yelled a hunting cry, Valentine would not have thought it misplaced. On and on they rode. The bay began to falter and would not last much longer. How much further? Valentine noted Blackie showed no sign of slackening pace.

The path swung south, breakers fading behind them. Ahead lay the ghostly stretches of beach known as Seal Sands. The gelding stumbled, then shambled into a jarring walk. Valentine cursed and kicked free of the stirrups then slid to the ground. Instinct turned Richard John's head. Straight-legged, he hauled back to curb his mare's gallop and she went down on her haunches, sliding to a standstill. Upright, shaking out her mane,

Blackie turned back to where Valentine was holding the gelding's head.

"He's lamed," he said, looking up.

"No matter. Leave him." Richard John extended a hand so Valentine could swing up behind onto Blackie's broad rump. "We're almost there. Someone'll collect him later." He urged the mare into a mile eating canter, the gelding left standing on trembling legs with neck bowed as they vanished into the night. But even the powerful mare was almost blown. Head held low, mouth foaming, the pattern of her hooves grew ragged. After five minutes Richard John slackened the reins and she slowed gratefully to a walk, ribs heaving. Looking over John's shoulder, Valentine could see a hovel half buried in the sandbanks, built of gnarled and bleached drift wood.

"Jacko, you lazy good for nothing!" John shouted, gesturing for Valentine to dismount. On foot, they approached the hut. "Come out, Jacko, or I'll come in and dig you out of your pit!"

"Who be there? Who be dragging an old man out in the dead of night?" A hunched figure emerged, struggling into a ragged coat, scratching at unkempt hair and beard, both grey. "Why," he chuckled. "If it's not Mr John. No, my old eyes lie. Why would Mr John be riding on the wrong side of the river at this time of night? I can't see no badger hounds..."

"Enough fooling, Jacko. I need your boat and quickly."

"Well, Mr John, I don't rightly know..."

"If you get a move on there's a gold guinea in it for you."

The old man's eyes lit up. "Most generous, to be sure."

Richard John laughed. "You won't think so when you know what I want you to do."

*   *   *

At the estuary mouth, the River Tees was almost three and a half miles wide, a spider's web of half navigable channels and inlets, the main channel fraught with shoaling water and ever-shifting sandbanks at the whim of wind and tide. It was a long hard pull across choppy water, battling the flowing tide. Without Jacko's expertise they would have grounded time and again or been carried away. The old man was wise in the ways of the river and much stronger than he looked. He worked the starboard oar while Valentine pulled on the port side. Exertion insulated him from the wind whipping off the water, bitter enough to cut through the toughest material. Richard John huddled in the sternsheets, coat tight about his shoulders. His face was lined, age showing, strength drained by their escape. Now and again he cursed Jacko, urging him on, but it seemed he only spoke to remind them of his presence, a passenger for the back-breaking haul across the endless river.

When Valentine looked over his shoulder for nearly the hundredth time, a faint band of grey showed against the shifting black of the running current. It had to be the shore. He glanced at Jacko who merely nodded, then the boat scraped onto the beach, oars slopping in inches of oily water.

"Thank God," Richard John muttered, struggling to his feet and stepping gingerly along the rocking coble. He pushed between the two oarsmen, then climbed over the gunwale into the river. He turned and tossed a coin. "Here's your guinea, Jacko. When you get back over, the bay gelding's gone lame not far from your hut. When it's light, take both horses to the inn near the ferry. The landlord there knows what to do."

Jacko touched his forelock with a grin. "No sooner said than done." He winked as Valentine vaulted over the side. "Give us a shove off, boyo. Be seeing you..."

Richard John was waiting up the beach where the line of marram grass waved slender fingers at the river. When he saw Valentine was following, he tackled the first dune. At the crest he staggered, then righted himself. He crossed the lip and stumbled into the hollow where the wind was easier. He stopped, head bowed, then sank down onto the soft sand. Valentine came up behind him, then stretched a hand down to his shoulder.

"Are you ill?"

Richard John grimaced, a hand rubbing at his waistcoat. "A pain in my chest." He snorted a dry laugh. "What a time to pick. When we need all the speed we can get."

"What shall I do?"

John winced as a spasm gripped him, then shrugged it away. "You know Marsh House? Not far beyond the dunes? The farmer there will lend us two horses to get home." He forced a half smile. "He's another one that owes me. You go. When you get back the pain will have passed."

"You're sure?"

"It's always passed before, why not this time?"

Marsh House was gloomy and grey, standing foursquare in the midst of a sea of dunes more fitted for saltpans than farming. The tenant's face bade little welcome, but the name Richard John brought his features alive. Within minutes Valentine was mounted on a piebald, the lead rein of a strawberry roan in his hand. He waved goodbye and retraced his tracks. Richard John was still sitting in the lee of the dune, shoulders hunched.

"How bad is it?"

The pain was evident by his expression. "I can ride, if that's what you mean. Give me a hand." He raised an arm, the other pressed across his chest, fist clenched. Valentine hauled him up, placed his foot in a stirrup then put his shoulder under the older man's backside and heaved. For a moment John lay across the roan's neck, then eased his right leg over and sat up, gasping. "We must get home quickly," he said.

"No, we'll ride to Coatham," Valentine decided.

Richard John frowned. "What's on your mind?"

"No time to explain. Let's ride." He could see John was too

tired and in too much pain to argue, but he was sure the older man would have readily agreed if he had told him his idea. It was impossible to expect John to ride the six or seven miles to Saltburn without a rest.

When Valentine began to lead the way through the maze of dunes he was suddenly aware that the mantle of command had passed from the older man's shoulders to his own. Even more surprising was that he liked the feeling.

West Coatham stood only half a mile from the River Tees where the grey of the marsh grass became succulent green, able to support livestock. The village was hardly more than a single street parallel to the shore but divided from the tideline by a rolling ocean of dunes topped by coarse seagrass permanently stooped to face inland.

As they rode, Valentine glanced often at Richard John who was growing progressively more haggard. Slumped in the saddle, his body rolled in rhythm with the roan's even canter. But as they turned into West Coatham's High Street, the two horses slowing to a walk, he made a conscious effort to straighten his back, green eyes forced alert, lips pressed together. He eased the roan alongside the piebald, voice barely audible over the clicking of hooves on the rough shod street.

"What are you up to, lad?" The question cost him a measure of his remaining strength.

"We'll pay the king's boatman a visit." Valentine counselled. "Your watch has stopped and we want to know the time. Just make sure he gets a good look at us both, and ask him to repeat the time." Richard John stared at him, then nodded resigned.

At the far end of the street, beyond the well lit inn, the fishermen's cottages showed barely the glow of candlelight from curtained windows. Outside the last house Valentine leaned down from the saddle to rap his knuckles on the door.

"Yes, I'm coming," grumbled a voice after a second tattoo. The door cracked and a thick set man held up a storm lantern to examine the two riders. He looked again, carefully at the strawberry roan's rider. "Mr John, isn't it?" he scowled. "What do you want?"

Richard John pulled a gold hunter from his waistcoat pocket and feigned annoyance. "My watch has stopped. Can you oblige us with the hour?"

"That all?" The boatman rummaged in a pocket then pulled out a battered timepiece. "It's five minutes past eleven o'clock."

Richard John leaned over, cupping a hand about his ear. "Eh? What did you say?"

"He said five past eleven," Valentine commented.

"Yes, that's right. Five after eleven," the boatman confirmed.

"Thank you. We'll bid you goodnight." Richard John waved and turned the roan's head, coaxing the horse back along the street. When the door slammed shut, his shoulders slumped again. Valentine drew level to give support. The charade had cost the older man dearly. His eyes were squeezed shut as he rode, right hand clutching his shirt front. "Must get home," he muttered.

"That doesn't matter now. We can find you somewhere to rest for a while. One of the inns maybe?"

The smuggler's eyes flickered. "The Red Lion at Redcar. It's not far."

"Another one that owes you?"

Richard John attempted a smile and failed. Instead he concentrated on staying in the saddle. They walked the horses to Redcar, the next fishing village. A row of tumbledown single storey dwellings backed onto the landward side of the High Street and in the centre of these stood a large hostelry. The front of the Red Lion Inn was limewashed pristine white, but below the sign bearing a lion rampant and the cluster of mullioned windows, the rude paving was knee deep in wind driven sand.

The rear of the coaching inn was sheltered and the yard smelt of warm hay and manure. The cobbles rang with steel shod hooves then Richard John dismounted slowly at the old mounting block. He waited while Valentine turned the animals into an unoccupied loose box, then leaned heavily on his arm as they threaded through the parked coaches and carriages. Inside, the warm glow of a log fire offered welcome. Richard John sank onto a couch, head drooping. Valentine called for service.

"It's late, gentlemen," the innkeeper muttered, stalking across the room, wiping his hands on an apron. "Unless you're wanting a bed for the night?"

Richard John lifted his head. "Brandy."

The innkeeper became solicitous. "Mr John, I didn't see you. Forgive me. But are you all right? You're not looking yourself."

"Brandy, quickly," Valentine interrupted.

"I think he ought to lay down. I'll tell the missus..."

Richard John waved a hand. "No room."

"If you say so." His gaze ranged over Valentine's obviously good quality but travel stained suit. "And brandy for you too, sir?"

"Yes, but quickly." Valentine leaned forward. John's face was pale as death, green eyes sunken under furrowed brows. More alarming were his lips. Valentine remembered his father's advice. Blue lips and chest pains meant heart trouble. When John's eyes flickered toward him, he erased concern and offered a smile. "A rest and you'll be good as new."

John shot him a withering glance, then accepted a glass from the innkeeper's tray. He held it between shaking hands, sipping then sighing as the fire burned down through his chest to slacken the pain's hold.

"Only the best, Mr John," the innkeeper promised.

"Fetch another, if you please," Valentine ordered, to send the man away. He glanced at the lounge's other occupants but they were all attending to their own affairs. After the chill of the night, especially the river crossing, he thought he would relish the roaring fire, but now he was stifled and longed to be outside.

After three brandies the blue had left John's lips and colour was beginning to rise in his cheeks. His eyes had rekindled some of their green fire and his shoulders seemed less hunched. Valentine realised the mantle of power was shifting again, the older man reclaiming it. He was content to wait and give John time to recover. He sipped his own brandy, a stranger to the spirit, more used to ale and the occasional tot of rough gin. John remained broody, hands cupped about his glass. When the landlord ordered more logs for the fire, glancing over at their table, Valentine made an excuse to tend the horses in order to escape for a few minutes. When he returned Richard John looked up.

"I won't die on you tonight, lad."

Valentine smiled. "I never thought you would. It'll pass, you said."

"I'm not always right. If I was I wouldn't have been caught on the beach tonight."

"But you suspected. That's why you kept me off the beach."

"Aye, that's so. And you did a good job."

"I did what I had to do," Valentine admitted. "That's all."

John shook his head then chuckled. "It was the way you did it. When you came into the shed you looked desperate. A regular highwayman." When Valentine said nothing John patted his arm. "No, you did well. Especially at Coatham. My brain wasn't working. You learn quickly." His eyes raked the younger man's features. "Perhaps too quickly. I could have done something with you at one time ..." He sighed, wistful. "...but it's too late now. I think it's all over."

"What?"

"The days of the free traders. Mark my words. When the war with the French is over, the men who matter in London are going to stamp out smuggling."

"The war might last years. We've always fought the French."

"True. But how much longer? Another five, ten or maybe even fifteen years at the very outside before Napoleon is beaten. But then it will happen. Those men in London hate us. We deprive them of revenue, and they know our money keeps Napoleon's soldiers on the march."

Valentine frowned. "How?"

"The little Frenchman needs gold to pay his armies. All his plundering and looting can't supply enough. English smugglers spend almost 10,000 guineas every week in the channel ports. And they pay in gold. So on the high seas French frigates attack any English ship of war, but our luggers have free access to French ports under their very noses. Courtesy of M'sieur Boney."

"I can't see the truth in that."

"It's true. Money makes the world go round. Nothing else. Even war doesn't get in the way. And wars are about money anyway." Richard John smiled sardonically. "Even crazier, His Britannic Majesty's Navy will fight the French to the death, yet the Lords of the Admiralty in London get a regular supply of the best French contraband brandy." He plumbed the depths of his glass, drained it then motioned for another. "But when it suits them, the end will come. My name is on the cards already."

"What makes you say that?"

"Too many things have gone wrong lately. Ah, I'm an old man. I should have given it up a long time ago. I would have too, but for my son. Tom thinks of naught but hounds and hunting. So here I am. Well, sunset be glory."

Valentine frowned. "Sunset be glory? I don't understand."

John pursed his lips. "Something my father used to say. It means that the end should be as a man should end. He should die with his boots on." He laughed bitterly. "But for a successor, I would have died in bed like an old woman." His green eyes focused into a penetrating gaze on his young companion's face. "A few years back, you could have been that man."

Valentine looked puzzled.

"You like my daughter?" John asked.

Valentine blushed. "Margaret? I..."

John nodded. "I can see you do."

"But what of your business?"

"There may be time enough yet for you to make a hatful of money before it's all over. Then you can do what you like." He gestured to the surroundings. "An inn, or some other business. Whatever you want." He touched Valentine's sleeve, rubbing the cloth between his fingers. "Money buys quality, yet what is important is the quality of your life, not how much money you have. Do you understand?"

"No," Valentine admitted.

"One day you will," Richard John promised.

*   *   *

The coastal track from Redcar turned eastward past outlying farms and wound over the flat coastal plain. On the left stood Marske Hall, a replica of a Jacobean country house. A broad edifice of sandstone with numerous leaded windows that looked impressive in the village, yet small for the country seat of a man as wealthy as Lord Dundas. Lights shone in several of the downstairs rooms.

As they rode by, now at a slower pace so they could talk, Richard John looked at the house with a sneer. "Another one out for my blood, I fear. Once a valued customer, now he buys less than a farm servant. Do you know, I've done him more service than he deserves. When his daughter was being courted by Earl Fitzwilliam, who do you think supplied her bottom drawer? Who else in war-torn England could have procured bolts of silk and Flemish lace, handkerchiefs and gowns, pretty things by the score, even a spinning wheel? There's a tax on them too, you know, lad. And Lord Dundas? He was never short of spirits or tobacco. Even tea and chocolate to tease his wife's palate. And his guests pass hours at whist using playing cards I provided. Without the luxuries I broke the law to bring him, his life would be a misery." He snorted. "But would he allow me into the drawing room to meet his guests? No, yet he asks me graciously if they may hunt with my hounds." He spat into the hedgerow. "Aristocracy, bah. Dunderheads mostly, with the manners of pigs and the morals of alleycats. You know what the aristocracy are?"

Valentine clucked to his piebald horse, knowing no answer was expected.

"Let me tell you," Richard John continued. "They are nothing. Everybody bows and scrapes to them, me included at one time, but I'll bow no more. William The Conqueror, you know, always signed his name 'William the Bastard' because he was illegitimate. A fitting leader. When he invaded England, looting and murdering to take the crown, he divided the country up between his friends, the Norman warlords. That's what the aristocracy is descended from, murderers and looters, their dark deeds committed in the name of warfare. Legal murder. And now their descendants think themselves better than you and me. The irony, of course, is they're so particular they won't let their daughters or sons marry outside the circle of nobility. The dividend for that is half their children are dribblers and idiots. That's the aristocracy for you."

Valentine stared at him.

Richard John caught his eye and gave a crooked smile. "Have I shocked you, lad? You will learn. There may be a measure of respect, often grudgingly given, but really everybody despises everyone else. Everyone who is not like themselves. And we're all competitors in this great game of life."

*   *   *

"We were beginning to think you weren't coming home," Sarah-Anne Rudd chided as she placed porridge on the breakfast table. It was still night outside, corners of the sky greying with the coming dawn.

"Where's Dad?" Valentine asked his step mother.

"He's off already. He said there would be mackerel running in after sprats as the tide flows."

Valentine nodded as he spooned the oatmeal into his mouth. He pictured *Rebel Maid*, his dad sitting on the stern thwart, hand on the tiller as he watched the lugsail draw, the lee gunwale skimming inches above the glassy sea, mysterious with the hope of a good day's fishing. He abandoned the image as he wolfed down the remainder of his breakfast, then pushed the dish away. He smiled his satisfaction, watching Sarah-Anne busy at her range.

She had aged gracefully, her face still carrying lines of good breeding but now joined by the wear of hard years. Her hands read poverty, nails broken and skin cracked. She had no servants now to handwash all the clothing or scrub the doorstep or the thousand other jobs a woman did to take proper care of her home and family. He thought of Richard John's house with its cook and kitchen maids. His wife's hands weren't chapped and raw. Money, that was all it took. Fishing might bring pleasure, but it was a hard way to make a living. No man got rich putting off in a coble each day. Time spent with Richard John made him realise it was using your head that made you rich; that and a few risks.

His stepmother turned from her work and smiled, eyes fastened on his face. Sitting there at the table, hands across his stomach, he looked so like his father had looked twenty years before. The same craggy features and warm brown eyes. That slightly curling brown hair long enough to brush his collar. She remembered how slim his father had been when she met him. Years of hearty eating had expanded his stomach until he was heavily built, a powerful man. Oh, how her life had changed the moment she first saw him at Scarborough. The parsonage where she had been brought up seemed a world away from the life she had chosen with Jackie in a tiny fisherman's cottage on the seashore. A life of making do and mend, but although her purse was empty, her heart was full. Her family was her whole life. They carried their love for each other with an easy nonchalance, but shown in their care of each other, father, step mother and son.

Now the little boy she had first befriended was fast becoming a man. The day was near when he would flee the nest to make his own life, but the knowledge did little to ease the pain. She had no idea what had happened that night on the beach a few weeks ago, only there had been trouble. She had worried when he did not return home, although they'd had a message he was fine. She had been amazed at the story of his recuperation at Cliff House and Richard John's concern for him. What could Valentine have that remotely interested the smuggler?

"You say he was drunk?" Sarah-Anne asked.

"Yes. We had a hard ride from Hartlepool and he needed a rest. He drank brandy, for medicinal purposes." Valentine shrugged. "And one glass led to another."

Her eyes were steely, inquisitive. "Why were you at Hartlepool?"

"Mr John was buying some horses," he lied. "I got him home and the maids carried him to bed."

She eyed his suit, her hands kneading dough on the scrubbed table. "And where did you get such fine clothes?"

He averted his gaze. "Mr John gave me them. My own got torn and he wanted me to look respectable when we went to do business..." A soft knocking saved him. He bounded to his feet. Roland Flounder was on the step. He grinned as he entered the room, nodding to Sarah-Anne who gestured with a floury hand to a chair.

"What've you been up to, then?" Roland asked eagerly.

Valentine glanced at his stepmother then back. "This and that. How'd you know I was here?"

Roland made a face. "A little bird. And that's not all." He

punched his friend's arm. "What's this about a certain lass?"

Sarah-Anne's head came up a fraction before she brought the reaction under control and stared fixedly down at the dough. *The day is coming faster than I expected,* she thought.

"No less than Margaret John herself, eh?" Roland continued, oblivious to Valentine's warning frown. "But you're the sly one."

"It's not like that," Valentine blurted, colouring. "Anyway, more important things afoot." He glanced again at his stepmother to make sure she wasn't watching, then jerked his head at the door. "Fancy a walk? I could use some fresh air." He was out of his seat, tugging Roland's sleeve. "See you later, Ma."

Sarah-Anne lifted her head and smiled. "Your dad'll be back before noon. I think he'd like to talk to you."

"I'll be back," he promised, following Roland to the door. Outside, they walked toward the beach. "I heard about Tommy getting caught on a fence on the cliff..."

Four men stepped out to block their path. Valentine and Roland froze, scanning the features above the scarlet jackets with white crossbelts, three-cornered hats set low, shading dark eyes. One bearing three stripes on his arm tilted his head.

"Valentine Rudd?"

"Yes?"

The sergeant pulled out a sheet of parchment then slowly unfolded it to hold aloft. "I have a warrant for your arrest."

Valentine was rooted. He stared hard at the Dragoon, then abruptly turned to look back. In the cottage doorway his stepmother was standing, face blanched. Flour covered hands hung useless by her sides, shoulders slumped. Unable to utter a word, Valentine turned back to face the Dragoons. Every one of them was smiling grimly, triumph written in their eyes.

The sergeant waved a casual hand. "Take him," he ordered.

SEVEN

Frederick, Lord Dundas, was a heavy man of large appetites; in his youth women and hunting, and now in later years, drinking and eating. Presiding over Guisborough courthouse, he sat as Chairman of the Magistrates Bench, hands spanning a generous paunch, thumbs tucked in his waistcoat pockets. Ruddy faced like a farmer, shuddering jowls hung in folds over his stiff collar. His eyes were once so sharp he could sight a partridge put to flight before the rest of the line could snap shut their shotguns. Now short sighted, he had developed a habit of tilting his head down to stare over the top of his pince-nez spectacles when making a point. Until now he had sat back, unable to restrain the impatience which turned down his mouth. He swivelled his gaze to take in his two companions, one either side, then leaned forward to glower at the clerk seated below him. He decided to dispense with his services.

"Silence there in the gallery or I'll have you all ejected." He sniffed, pince-nez twitching, as the courtroom spectators subsided, then waved a limp wrist at the stand. "The witness may proceed, but for God's sake, get on with it."

In the dock, Richard John's foot touched Valentine's and the youth saw the smuggler smirk briefly. On the witness stand, the Riding Officer looked uncomfortable under the bench's collective scrutiny. His coal black eyes skittered from face to face then to the crown's prosecution lawyer who urged him on with a curt nod. Fingering his starched collar, he touched a scrap of paper clinging to his jaw line, a reminder of morning carelessness with the razor.

"Well?" Lord Dundas rumbled, jowls shaking.

Hardiman's lips squeezed into a bloodless line to stifle his embarrassment. He blinked rapidly then leaned forward on the balls of his feet as though ready to plunge in. "Well, m'lord ..."

"Your worship," the clerk of the court corrected him.

Confused, Hardiman frowned, staring blankly.

"His worship may actually be a lord," the clerk reminded him pedantically, "but when Lord Dundas is sitting as chairman of the bench you address him as 'Your worship'."

"What? Yes. Thank you." The Exciseman took another deep breath. "Your worship. After Officer Billington and myself apprehended the perpetrators on the beach at Hartlepool, they was conveyed by box wagon under escort to Stranton brickworks where they was incarcerated under lock and key in the soaking shed. A Dragoon was detailed to guard them. Officer Billington and myself retired to the office to await the return of the main body of soldiers who was proceeding with the collection of contraband brought illegally ashore..."

"You're saying these two men were arrested on the beach?" Dundas asked.

"No, sir. Only Richard John."

Dundas raised an eyebrow. "Then the other prisoner is not an alleged smuggler?"

"No sir. Or at least not..."

"Very well. Go on."

"After a period of time elapsed, the door of the office was opened and we was forced at gunpoint to unlock the soaking shed wherein the apprehended smugglers was released and we was tied up and left."

"Who held you at gunpoint?" the prosecution lawyer prompted.

"The second prisoner, sir. Valentine Rudd." Hardiman shot a look of pure hatred at the dock.

"But he's naught but a lad," Dundas commented.

Hardiman's eyes narrowed as he pointed a shaking finger across the courtroom. "He's tried to kill me once, and he'll try again!"

The defence solicitor jumped to his feet. "I strongly object to the last statement. The fact the accused allegedly pointed a pistol at the officer does not imply he would have fired it. And if the witness is referring to another incident, then a previous alleged assault has no bearing on this case..."

"Yes, yes, you may be aspiring to silk, Mr James, but you're not at the Quarter Sessions now," Lord Dundas said dryly. "We take your point. Officer Hardiman, please confine yourself to relevant facts, not wild accusations."

The crown's lawyer came to his feet in a bid to avert the bench's impatience. "Officer Hardiman, when you apprehended the smugglers on the beach, you recognised one of them?"

"Yes." The Exciseman nodded. "I saw him immediately."

"Do you see him in this courtroom? If so, can you indicate him?"

Hardiman's gaze swivelled to the dock and he raised an accusing finger. "It was him. Richard John. That man sitting there."

Counsel nodded. "Very well. And when you and Officer Billington were taken prisoner, what was the lighting like in the office?"

Hardiman pursed his lips, hands on the rail. "Very good. Two lamps. One hanging on the ceiling and one on the table."

"You are saying, in fact, there is no possibility you are mistaken as to the identity of your captor?"

"None at all."

"If he is in this courtroom, can you point him out?"

Hardiman nodded emphatically. "Yes, he is in the dock next to Richard John."

The prosecutor smiled. "Thank you. No further questions, your worship."

"Would the defence care to cross-examine?" asked the clerk of the court.

"No questions at this time, your worship."

Lord Dundas ignored the clerk's frown as he leaned forward. "Is that wise, Mr James?"

The defence counsel rose to his feet. "We believe our first witness will dispense with the need for further questioning of this officer, your worship. We do not intend to waste the bench's time further. If it pleases the court, we should like to call the first defence witness."

Dundas leaned back, curious. He gestured with a limp wrist. "Very well, continue."

Valentine was transfixed by the scene in the court. The lawyers and magistrates were jockeying for position to score points off each other in some kind of elaborate game. Using words to do battle was their strength and the knowledge of the law was their armoury, just as his own was familiarity with the ways of the sea while Richard John's was in striking bargains and organising. Yet, while the men of the law were fastidiously polite to each other, leaving him and his patron as onlookers – onlookers with the threat of prison sentences hanging over their heads – Valentine suddenly understood that justice had nothing to do with what was happening here. What was important to these lawyers was winning, not guilt or innocence. In which case the winner would be the best lawyer, the one with the keenest mind and the subtlest of tongues provided he had a few solid facts. And the best came most expensive. Richard John could afford the best – Mr William James. Valentine was grateful for that. He switched his attention back to the witness box.

"...the whole truth, and nothing but the truth, so help me God."

"Please state your name, residence and occupation," the clerk ordered. The witness took his hand from the bible then looked from the clerk to the bench, then out at the court.

"Michael Cummins, sir, of High Street, West Coatham. I am a fisherman by trade."

Mr William James smiled to put his witness at ease. "You say you are a fisherman. Do you ever take work from anybody else?"

"I do, sir. When I'm asked, I work as an auxiliary boatman for the Excise."

"Under whose orders?"

"Why, Officer Hardiman, stationed at Marske. Before him, I took orders from Officer Grey, then stationed at Redcar."

"So, you've been given occasional employment by the Excise service over a number of years?"

Cummins rubbed a grizzled chin. "Five and a half, or six."

"Were you working the night before last? Tuesday?"

"No sir, I was at home."

James smiled. "Did you have any callers that night?"

"Yes sir, I did. Two men on horses knocked on my door to ask the time. It was five past eleven."

"Are you certain of that?"

Cummins nodded positively. "Yes, sir, I am. One of the men did not hear me and asked me to repeat it. Five past eleven o'clock."

"Did you see the two men clearly?"

"Yes, I was carrying a lantern. I held it up to their faces and recognised one of them. I remember being surprised it was Mr John from Saltburn." When the lawyer frowned, Cummins pointed to the dock. "That gentleman. And the young one there was with him."

James smiled. "Thank you." He turned toward the bench. "Your worships. With respect, I should like to submit that if my clients were in West Coatham at five past eleven o'clock that night, it is impossible for them to have been at Hartlepool where the alleged offences took place on the same evening."

Lord Dundas frowned, then consulted the two other magistrates on the bench. After a moment he nodded then leaned forward again. "Would both counsel approach the bench." The prosecution lawyer rose and joined his opponent in front of the magistrates. Dundas glowered at him. "Were you aware of this evidence?"

"No, your worship."

"Was a Notice Of Alibi served?"

"No, your worship. My learned friend informed me the witness would appear, but not the precise nature of his testimony."

"Tut tut, Mr James," Dundas rebuked before addressing the prosecution lawyer again. "Do you dispute it would be impossible to travel from Hartlepool to Coatham in the time between the incident and the time the boatman testified?"

The lawyer reluctantly shook his head. "No, not if the witness is to be believed."

"Are you accusing him of perjury?" Dundas asked mildly, eyebrows raised.

"No, no, of course not, your worship."

James stepped into the void. "I can also produce the landlord of the Red Lion Inn who can testify he served both my clients shortly after eleven that night."

Dundas nodded. "Even by the shortest route, the journey from Hartlepool to the ferry, and then from the landing could not have been accomplished even if they had ridden racehorses. To continue this hearing would be fruitless. It may be a *prima facie* case but their alibi is undoubtedly sound. They could not have been in both places at once. You agree?"

The prosecution lawyer nodded curtly. "Yes, your worship."

Lord Dundas eyed him then raised his voice so all in the courtroom could hear. "The bench finds there is lack of evidence." Dundas lowered his head and peered over his pince-nez spectacles at the defendants in the dock. He sniffed once. "Case dismissed," he pronounced.

*   *   *

"He was lucky, that's all," Michael Cummins said as he stood on the courtroom steps, gazing over the roofs of Guisborough. Smoke rose from a few chimneys to blur the view down to the Priory arch but there was plenty of traffic moving toward the weekly market in Northgate.

"Luck be damned," Hardiman growled, stuffing tobacco into his pipe to occupy restless hands. "They're all in league, John and the bloody squires."

"But I saw them that night. I told no lies," Cummins stated.

Hardiman shook his head in disbelief. "So you say. Well, I don't know how that sly old fox did it, but he did. Now, don't you worry, Richard John'll get his. And that arrogant young bastard sitting with him. I'll get him if it's the last thing I do."

Cummins frowned. "What's he to you?"

"Rudd? He made me look a bumbling fool in there. Sneaking into the office and holding Billington and me at gunpoint. And that was the second time. At Saltburn a few weeks ago he nearly killed me. Brought me down from my horse. I can only thank God his pistol misfired, but my face still pains me where he hit me, and to cap it all he stole my cutlass. They'll deduct that from my salary. At least with Richard John it's purely business, but that young bastard has made it personal. Tries to murder me, then has the cheek to draw a pistol on me again and get away with it in court." He drew out his pipe and spat on the steps. "Next time he won't even reach the court. I'll murder him with my bare hands before those squires set him free again. And that's no threat," Hardiman stated. "I'll swing for the bastard."

"And a 'good morning' to you, Officer."

He looked round at Richard John emerging from the court with Valentine Rudd and the lawyer William James. Eyes thunderous, Hardiman sneered at the trio. "A good day for some."

Richard John feigned innocence before producing a brittle smile. "We all have our days." He turned to the others who were watching the Exciseman. "Don't we, Valentine?"

"Some have more days than others," Valentine commented, staring Hardiman in the eye. "A good day to you, Officer," he concluded, then they moved past, descending the steps to a waiting coach.

"You're right there, laddo," Hardiman muttered as the driver whipped the horses into a trot and the coach pulled away. "And you might have less days left than most."

*   *   *

"Do you want to see your mother?"

Valentine drew his gaze from the fields and glanced at Richard John who sat beside him on the hard leather seat of the jolting coach. "I'll visit her later and explain. It was only a case of mistaken identity."

John laughed and slapped his companion's knee. "I suppose there's a young lady you'd rather talk to first." His eyes glinted mischievously, almost as though he wasn't talking about his own daughter.

At the mention of Margaret, Valentine's stomach turned over. Now the court business was over, she was foremost in his mind. He could picture her as clearly as if she was sitting opposite in the coach. Her smooth skin, throat soft and inviting, hair fresh and silky. He looked down at his hands, fingers splayed across his knees. They longed to touch her, to caress the hollow of her back and his body ached for her slender arms enfolding him, soft breasts flattened against his chest, thighs hotly pressing against his. He sucked his teeth. His lips desired the taste of hers, hungry yet yielding. Ah, but that would be the day. If only she wanted him too...

"You hear me?" the old smuggler quizzed then roared with laughter. "It's love. I'd forgotten what it's like. One mention of her and you're in a trance. Be damned, but she's a good looking girl, even if I say so myself." His laugh died abruptly. "But lad, never hurt her." He stared for a moment, then sighed. "I'd hurt you more than you could ever think possible."

*   *   *

Richard John threw open the coach door and stepped down onto the gravel drive. He stood, hands on hips, surveying Cliff House. By God, it was good to be free. For a moment in the court he had wondered if Lord Dundas was under instruction from some higher authority to lock him up. If so, the bench would have totally discounted the boatman's evidence, claiming the alibi had been bought by bribery. Thank God the lad had taken him to the Red Lion as well. He wondered if it had been by accident or design. Either way, it had probably saved them. There were too many witnesses to disprove. Valentine stooped as he climbed down to stand with him. The more he studied the boy, the more he liked him.

"I want to talk to you later. In my study." When Valentine nodded, Richard John turned and scanned the house. Was there nobody to welcome them home? A groom dressed in old trousers and a collarless shirt emerged from the stable block to help the driver unharness the team.

"Welcome home, sir," he grinned.

"Have you seen Miss Margaret?"

The groom ducked the wheel horse's snapping teeth and glanced over his shoulder. "Blaze is missing from his stall, so it's likely Miss Margaret is riding with Master Tom. His hunter's out too. I know Master Tom likes to ride along the cliff..."

A rumble of hoofbeats turned their eyes to the lodge gate. A black pony marked by a white blaze down its face and three white socks cantered into the drive. Margaret rode him, hair streaming in the wind, a crop waving over her head. In her tracks rode Tom, holding a bay hunter down to an easy canter. His expression betrayed no pleasure. The black pony skidded to a halt, hooves grinding the gravel. Margaret flung herself from the saddle into Richard John's arms, breathless.

"We were out on Huntcliff when we saw the coach and I forced Tom to turn back," she panted. "I knew they must have found you not guilty. I've been watching for you all morning. I thought you'd never come home."

Hands about her waist, Richard John looked down into her eyes of Caribbean blue and it was as if all the light of the sun was channelled into a beam which lit up her face. Hair tangled by the wind, cheeks flushed, her lips were damp and luscious. She had never looked more beautiful, and he had never been so proud she was his daughter.

"So the fox and the cub shook off the pack," Tom commented dryly. Valentine looked up. Tom John sat the hunter as though part of the saddle. He carried a bone handled crop whose lash tickled the gravel by the horse's hooves. He stared for a moment at his father. "The old fox is sly indeed. Caught in the hen coop, he uses his cub to make the hounds switch scent. Very clever."

Valentine could read Tom's hatred of his father, perhaps some jealousy too. Although Valentine had only met Tom a few times at Cliff House, Tom's manner was always condescending, and any reference to the way Richard John's living was earned was jeered, as though making money, or even discussing it, was a vulgar subject. Valentine found Tom both ungrateful and irritating. He resented Tom being offered every chance in life, yet squandering them with casual contempt. What he would give for half one of those opportunities. He glanced then at Margaret but all her attention was given to her father, smiling and laughing, and Richard John seemed oblivious to his son's remarks.

"Perhaps even you could learn a few tricks from the old fox," Valentine remarked bluntly.

Tom stared down, patronising. "You forget, cub, I am the hunter, not the quarry." He spurred the bay and swung its head toward the open fields. At the gallop within a second, the hunter leapt the paddock fence with an arrogant nonchalance, hooves kicked high, revelling in a moment's grace from the earth's gravity. Valentine watched the exhibition, cursing himself for failing to loose a parting volley. Angry, he looked at Margaret instead. She had stepped back to arm's length from her father. Her hacking jacket had fallen open and a white silk blouse did little to hide the thrust of her breasts. With a start, he realised she was not wearing a riding habit, but men's breeches. He stared at her shapely legs usually disguised by a skirt. He found the breeches both shocking and exciting. Both emotions tussled for superiority. Ashamed, he prised his gaze upward.

"I'm so glad you're home, father."

"Well, you can thank the lad here," Richard John said, to draw Valentine into their intimacy. Margaret glanced sideways for a moment, her eyes only meeting Valentine's for a split second.

"Thank you," she said tersely, then ignored him.

Richard John made a face over her head as though to say sorry, then touched her arm. "Anyway, Missy, I need a drink. Are you coming inside?"

"Of course," she beamed, locking her arm through his and turning toward the house. Richard John looked back over his shoulder.

"That talk, lad. My study in half an hour. You'd best go to the kitchen. I'm sure you can charm some dinner out of Mabel."

Valentine watched them walk away, Margaret on springy legs. The short hacking jacket revealed her rounded buttocks, twill breeches clinging to her flesh. But with the warm gush of desire came despair. At the last moment she flung her head round and treated him to a look which said she was well aware he had been watching. Blushing, he dropped his gaze and set off for the kitchen. At the door he caught something on the edge of his vision. A horse had turned in at the lodge gate and was trotting toward the house. He did not know the piebald, but he watched the rider dismount before he recognised him. It was the boatman from Marske, Michael Cummins, who had testified that morning in court. Curious...

*   *   *

Richard John was exasperated. He always knew Margaret was headstrong, and he reluctantly accepted some of the blame, having spoilt her as only fathers spoil daughters. If he didn't love her so much then she would make him as angry as Tom did. Draining his glass, he splashed more brandy into it, then sipped slowly, trying to organise his reasoning. But for everything he said she had a ready answer. He gazed at her across the desk. For a second all he could see was her mother, that day long ago when he had first come to Saltburn. God, she had been so beautiful she stole the words from his mouth and the breath from his lungs. He blinked and the vision faded.

"You could do worse," he repeated. "He's a bright lad, and he's not exactly ugly."

Margaret's mouth turned down. "Father, he's a fisherman. Do you want me to live in a little cottage and stink like a fish-wife?"

"I'd rather that than have you living in a great country house with some drooling half-wit as a husband."

"And this fisherman's not a half-wit, I suppose?" she sneered.

"He's resourceful and he's got courage, too." He grinned lop-sidedly, devious. "They say girls always marry men who are like their fathers."

Her eyebrows raised. "And he's like you?"

"More than you know. And if he's half as bright as I think he is, then he won't be a fisherman long. I'll see to that."

She nodded then. "I thought so. Mother saw it first. You're grooming him, aren't you? Tom turns you down flat, so the fisherman replaces him as heir apparent. And of course part of the legacy is your daughter's hand." Her face set into rigid defiance. "Well, I'll be the one to decide who I marry. Nobody else." She rose from her seat, ending the interview and strode across the room. Wrenching the door open she spun back to glare. "And I'll not marry a fisherman. I'll talk no more about it."

She turned then to leave and came face to face with Valentine who was waiting outside. Tossing her head, she stalked away down the passage. Valentine had heard nearly all the conversation. As she passed, his face burned and he had to wait for his colour to subside before knocking on the door.

Richard John was staring out of the window, nursing a brandy snifter. "Sit down, lad. Just as I came in, I had a visitor."

Valentine met his eyes. "The boatman?"

"You saw him? Yes, seems our local Exciseman has developed a rather strong dislike for you. Not only that but he's sworn to kill you rather than haul you up in court again. After Hartlepool, this morning in court put the cap on it."

"So what do I do?"

"You lay low here as you've been doing. You have my assurance you won't be bored." He smiled then and swung his chair round so he could place the empty glass on the desktop. He opened both hands and placed them face down on the scarred leather surface. "I know you can read and write. You say you know arithmetic too. Well, let me test you." He opened a drawer and pulled out a ledger, turning it round to face Valentine. "Add up this column and write the total at the bottom, like the previous page. There's a pen and ink there." He sat back and watched. Valentine was quick, and when he had finished he went back and checked his work. And the addition was correct. Another small point in his favour. He smiled when Valentine looked up. "You like arithmetic?"

Valentine was honest. "I don't know. I don't use it very much."

"Remember what I said? Money makes the world go round, and the first rule of making money is keeping track of it. For example, I lease fifty acres of land at Skelton Grange, further up the lane, and I have a farm manager who keeps ledgers so I always know the farm's financial state. I use a double entry system which means that everything is entered twice and is thus checked against itself. I keep other ledgers for my other business – private books. But these will serve us today." He leaned forward and bade Valentine draw up his chair. "I'll show you how it works."

He began to explain, occasionally stopping to question Valentine, only continuing when he was satisfied by the answers. Valentine grasped the fundamentals of book-keeping quickly and even Richard John was surprised when the boy began to think ahead, asking perceptive and penetrating questions. They began to discuss how the farm manager could hypothetically cheat his employer by making false entries. Richard John patiently explained that no matter how devious, at some point the books would always reveal the manager for a liar. "One thing to remember is that every employer expects to be cheated by his employees. A manager will probably steal hard cash or goods to be resold, but even a farm labourer will take home a turnip he's not entitled to. No matter what, employees will fiddle. To what degree is what is important. If he's competent and hard working and he fiddles a little, then that's better than a lazy, useless man who fiddles a lot. One can be compensated for... Yes?" he said irritably, interrupted by a knock at the door.

Mabel put her head into the room. "High tea is served, sir."

Richard John frowned. "Is that the time? The afternoon disappeared. We'll be in directly. Thank you, Mabel." When the door shut, he examined his pupil's face. "Three hours we've been talking. What with court this morning, it's been a long day."

Valentine was still alert. "I wasn't bored. It's interesting that figures can be juggled to balance, and that they can be made to show what you want them to show. But something puzzles me..."

"Whoa!" Richard John laughed, holding up his hands. "Ask me tomorrow morning. Ten o'clock in here, and we start lesson two. You're hungry? Stupid question. Young men are always hungry. Let's go and eat."

*   *   *

Valentine stood watching the helpers roust the pack from the kennels. The hounds tumbled over each other, eager for freedom. They milled in the yard, tails wagging, spilling over into the gravel drive before the whipper-in could call them together. The morning was fresh and while most hounds were already casting for non-existent scent lines on the ground, here and there a brindled dog stood tall, muzzle testing the day's fragrances in the hopes of a good day's hunting. Next to the stable block a groom was holding a bay hunter and Blaze, Margaret's pony, both saddled and glossy coated. Valentine knew this was his only opportunity to see her if he didn't want to wait until dinner that evening. She may not speak to him, but at least he could feast his eyes on her.

"They're my beauties."

Valentine turned to see Richard John gazing fondly at his hounds. "You know, lad, when we started, I bought couples from all the best kennels in the Northern Counties, even some from further afield. This pack are offspring from those original couples. Their breeding records are kept scrupulously. Magical names too; Blagdon Driver, Splender and Sebright, Harmony and Melody. Ah, when Melody begins to talk..." The sentiment in his voice rasped into irritation. "You wearing those breeches again, Missy?"

Margaret stood in the open doorway of the house and

Valentine's breath caught in his throat. "Father! Blaze jumps better when I wear them. My weight is more evenly distributed. And that's scientific."

Beside her, her brother Tom smacked the handle of his whip into an open palm. "What she means, is the men pay her more attention," he commented dryly with a sly glance at Valentine.

Richard John growled. "Whatever, I wish you'd wear a proper riding habit. But you're like your mother. No matter what I say, you'll do what you want."

Tom eyed his father's frock coat. "Not riding today?"

Richard John shook his head. "No, there's business to attend."

Tom shot a look at Valentine. "You've had business every morning for two weeks now. Locked up in your study. Are you teaching the cub to read and write, or is he teaching you to catch codling?"

His father's face hardened. "Son, if there was a race when they were handing out brains, then you didn't win it." He looked ready to say more, then turned instead to Margaret. "Just because a horse is bred from the finest blood stock doesn't mean it's got more sense than a plough horse." He touched her shoulder. "Plough horses have more stamina too. Now watch Blaze over the jumps." He looked back at his son who for once hadn't missed the point. "The meet's at Kirkleatham Hall? See if you can show the gentry a clean pair of heels when you chase." He patted both son and daughter. "Go on, away with you."

He watched them mount, Tom kicking his hunter into a trot and snapping at the whipper-in to walk the hounds, then Richard John glanced at Valentine. "You ride well. Would you rather be with them today?"

Valentine looked longingly at Margaret as she heeled Blaze into a canter, her cloud of blonde hair streaming about her shoulders. She made his heart ache. Nothing would have pleased him more than to ride with her all day. He tore his eyes away and looked to his patron. "No, I've things to learn before I enjoy myself."

Richard John stared, hearing the echo of his own lecture to Tom, then abruptly smiled. "Yes. Today we'll talk about profit and loss. How to achieve the former without suffering the latter. In my business it's all to do with buying and selling at the right price." He started for the house. "Everything has two prices; the buying price and the selling price. The difference between the two has to cover all your expenses, which are called the overheads, and there's also got to be some room for your profit. That's called the margin. All this is based on what you call a worthwhile return on your capital investment..."

As they mounted the steps to the house there was a crunching of hooves on the gravel and Blaze cantered up. Margaret hauled the pony to a standstill then kicked free of the stirrups, swung her leg over the pony's withers and slipped to the ground.

"What's the matter?"

"Nothing. I've changed my mind. I'm not hunting today."

"Why?"

"No reason. I just don't want to." She glared at her father. "Why do you do it? Why do you humiliate Tom so?"

"That's between him and me."

She raised an eyebrow. "Oh, is it? It's as if you prefer his company," she inclined her head at Valentine, "to your son's."

Richard John's face was grim. He was certainly not going to argue about it in front of Valentine. "There's nothing to discuss."

"I wouldn't understand, would I?" she sneered. "But then I'm only a girl. Very well, I won't ask you about it again." She dropped Blaze's reins and pushed past Valentine to the door.

"And what about your pony?" Richard John called after her. She stopped and swung back, contemptuously looking Valentine up and down.

"Let the fisherman stable him. He seems to be doing all your little jobs lately." Then she vanished into the hall. Richard John stared after her, but Valentine quickly grabbed Blaze's reins before the pony could wander.

Richard John grimaced. "You mind?"

Valentine stood at the pony's shoulder. "I'll be in shortly. I believe we were going to examine buying and selling margins." Richard John smiled then nodded mutely and followed his daughter into the house. Valentine ruffled the pony's mane, then touched the saddle where Margaret had been sitting only moments before.

It was still warm.

*   *   *

Hardiman tethered his black stallion to a sycamore within easy reach of good grazing. He unloaded his gear then shouldered his bag and set off toward the bottom of Saltburn Glen. It was leafy and cool, the beck rushing and tumbling in the distance, nearly a mile upstream from the beach. On the other side, hidden by trees, was Cliff House. Idly, he wondered what Richard John was doing. He certainly wasn't with the hunt. Hardiman had passed the hounds on the Marske Road, standing aside when Tom John and his helpers monopolised the road.

Then he shook his head. Why was he worrying about work when he had promised himself a day off to fish and relax. What with the area comptroller applying pressure, and his wife at that awkward time of the month when she nagged and cursed him non-stop, it made him wonder if life was worth enduring. Anything to get away from the house and find a little peace...

A red squirrel skittered up a tree trunk ahead. As he walked beneath, the splash of russet froze and he glanced up through the branches, dredging a rare smile. The woods evoked images of his youth. No responsibilities then, just the pursuit of enjoyment. Today I am going to do just that, he thought, working down the path below the canopy of oaks and elms, bird chatter sweet in his ears. He would wring every ounce of pleasure from his sport, or at best enough to warrant the bottle of contraband brandy Lord Zetland's gamekeeper had pocketed in exchange for fishing privileges.

Somewhere along here was a side path marked by... ah, there it was. It twisted down toward the beck, curling round a mound where a lightning-struck tree had fallen during a storm. The trunk now bridged the water, a tangle of roots frozen high in the air like the head of Medusa. Below, the stream had scoured the clay down to bedrock so on the other side of the water a wall of shale covered with lichen and moss rose up twenty or thirty feet. The top ledge was a jumble of vines and creepers, trees and shrubs, woven into a dense wall of vegetation making a natural fence along the rim. On this side, the track skirted the dead tree then swooped down the bankside into an arena of grass some fifty or sixty feet wide. A wide swathe of pebbles stretched from the bank, into shallow water on the inside of the curve, but it deepened to almost a yard where the trout weaved in and out of shadow by the reeds. It was warm in the hollow, too, wide enough so the canopy of trees opened to allow the sun to penetrate. In the middle of the grass arena lay a tree trunk, bark peeled smooth by several winters, an armchair provided by nature. It was his favourite spot.

Hardiman clumped down the path, sliding on the crumbling soil then made for the tree trunk. Sitting, he tamped tobacco into his pipe and lit it, then carefully baited his line. Ready, he paddled into the shallows and made a cast over the deep water. The lure landed on the surface, immediately drifting downstream with the current. When it threatened to snag in twisted roots hanging over the bend, he reeled in and cast again. After a while it became mechanical and he began to daydream.

Time seeped away, an hour then another as the trout refused

to bite, and hunger's subtle teeth began to gnaw at his stomach. He was wondering how much longer to wait before eating when he heard the stallion snicker up the bankside. He stiffened. It was a warning. Somebody was up in the trees behind him. The stallion snickered again. Hardiman was certain now. Casually, he reeled in then ambled out of the beck, boots squelching as he reached the tree. Stooping, he laid the rod down, a hand brushing his coat to check his pistol was hidden. He straightened up and walked slowly along the bank of the stream, fiddling with his fly buttons as though he was going to relieve himself. He knew there was a gap a few yards ahead where he could slip into the timber and work upwards and back to outflank whoever was out there.

Whoever it was, they would pay for ruining his sport.

*   *   *

Margaret shrugged off her silk blouse then pushed her thumbs into the back of her waistband and squirmed free of the riding breeches, tossing them onto the floor next to her boots for the maid to put away. She flicked through the contents of her wardrobe and chose a cotton dress. It felt deliciously light and loose on her skin after the figure-hugging twill of the breeches. She turned sideways in front of the mirror. Yes, it hung well, showing off her breasts and legs while disguising her bottom, undeniably her worst feature. Satisfied, she ran her hands through her hair, tilting her head this way and that to study her reflection. Not bad for a country girl. She grabbed a brush from the dresser and began to tug free the cotters tangled by the wind. The laborious process was somehow soothing as her hair regained its silkiness, and as she brushed, her anger seeped away.

Contrition's itchy fingers uncurled to pick at her conscience. She had been rather disrespectful to her father. She turned over their shouting match, held in front of that fisher lad. She knew she had been right in everything she had said, but there had been a look on her father's face momentarily revealing she had struck him deeply. She regretted it now.

She examined herself again, full face, then profile. She would have to apologise. The brief minute of embarrassment would be well rewarded. Father would become putty in her hands again. And she loved that feeling. With a laugh, she flicked her hips so the full skirt twirled about her legs, cool cotton caressing her calves, then slipped into a pair of soft shoes.

She almost danced down the staircase and along the hall toward the study. But outside the door she froze. Her father was talking to the fisher lad. Something about visiting the local inns and to meet some important people. Instantly, anger rose to kill her smile. She spun on her heel to walk away. The front door opened and her mother entered, carrying a basket of daffodils.

"Hello dear, I thought I'd gather a few for the sitting room. They're so pretty, don't you think?"

"Yes, very nice, mother." She pushed past, her mother frowning after her.

"Where are you going, dear?"

Margaret pouted. "Out. For a walk in the woods."

"Well don't forget lunch is in an hour."

"I won't!" Then she was gone, the door slamming behind her.

Once outside, Margaret angled toward the paddock, aiming for the fringe of trees that clothed the rim of Saltburn Glen. Inside the timber, the land fell away sharply, the clay bank keeping a tenuous grip on shrubs and saplings deformed by the bitter wind that scoured the Glen inland from the sea during winter months. At the bottom, Skelton Beck twisted and meandered toward the beach, almost half a mile distant. Margaret turned her back on the North Sea, instead following the beck toward Skelton Castle, invisible in the distance. She picked her way along the path worn by her father's pannier ponies, stepping round old droppings and where hooves had churned the soft track into glutinous mud. She did not look back once, shoulders set, silent.

She paid no attention to where she walked, thoughts churning, but always circling back to her father's preference for the company of that fisher lad instead of her brother's. And he even suggested she should think about letting him court her! She began to grow careless, stumbling here and there. When the path dipped sharply to the right, she lost her footing and began to slide. The beck scurried by only a yard away. The water was murky, deep, the pebble bed obscured. She slipped to the very lip of the bank, down on her left knee. She slithered to a halt, right shoe hanging motionless over the hurrying beck. She struggled to her feet, massaging her elbow where it had scraped along the ground. Irritated, she saw her dress was smeared with mud, but it was not important. She turned back to the path, doggedly following its tortured course.

Only when she reached where recent rains had washed out the bankside did she stop. She frowned at the heap of soft clay. Upover, a tangle of undergrowth was impassable, and downover lay only the beck. It wasn't too far to the other side and the water was shallow. She glanced down at her muddy dress. What difference would it make? Without further thought she tugged off her shoes, then picked her way down, gasping when she entered the icy stream. She tip-toed, teetering, one hand holding her shoes, the other clutching the dress hem. Uttering a little cry, she slipped, almost overbalancing, then scrabbled up the far bank, grass silky between her toes. Safe, she sat to catch her breath, then pulled on her shoes and began to walk again.

The path ran almost parallel to the one she had left, winding into the timber then easing back to the edge of the beck. A splash on her left startled her. A dark shadow snaked away under the surface. Trout. She laughed at herself, then continued walking, watching the ground ahead for roots and briars.

The tranquillity of the woods soaked into her conscious. The trees swaying gently, leaves rustling with the breeze, seemed to mock her black mood. It was as though they were murmuring how stupid it was to struggle when the sun was shining; that the earth was a good place, and that squabbles and bickering were a waste of valuable time. Life itself was what was important. It would only be as complicated as one made it.

She didn't even see the black horse until it snickered, hidden in the shadow of a wide branched sycamore. Her first thought was that it was Tom's hunter, then she saw it was a black stallion. She stepped forward for a closer look and the horse stretched its neck, snickering again and shaking its mane. She smiled, whispering, reaching a hand to pet it. The animal quietened, nuzzling her, shifting weight from hoof to hoof, tail switching at pestering flies. After a minute or two she patted it goodbye then resumed her walk.

When the hand shot out from behind a tree and grabbed her hair, reflex opened her mouth to scream. Only the cavernous barrel of a flintlock pistol choked off her scream as it appeared only inches from her face.

*   *   *

Hardiman worked his way back from the beck towards the stallion. Stealthy, pistol leading. he took great care as he checked then discounted possible approaches. His stomach turned over, adrenaline flooding his bloodstream, honing nerves and reactions. He reached the path, stepped quickly over it, expecting the crash of gunfire, but he knew he had to be above, not boxed against the beck. He sought the shadow of an oak, back so flat against the trunk he could feel the ridges of bark pressing through his coat.

What now? He tried to slow his breathing lest it be heard. Then he heard scuffling of feet on the path moving toward him.

Nerves peeled back his lips into a grimace. Soon. Soon. Now. He sprang out, a hand lunging for his assailant's throat, the other prodding the loaded pistol at chest height.

His hand closed, not on a throat, but on hair. His finger was tight on the trigger when he saw who he had captured. She stared at him wide-eyed, blood drained from her cheeks. His breath rushed out in a hiss of relief, but his hand still gripped her hair, forcing her face up. His eyes flickered beyond at the empty path. She was alone. Mouth open, her warm breath washed against his face as he stared down into her terrified eyes. His gaze travelled slowly down past her throat to the neckline of her dress. The thin cotton was little disguise for the soft curves of her breasts, rising and falling with fear.

"And what have we got here?" he asked, voice harsh. His killing rage dissipated swiftly, replaced by another even more basic urge. "Little Miss Margaret John, the old fox's untouchable daughter." He barked a laugh. He had come for a day's sport, but this would be better sport than fishing. All those times he had seen her and hungered to touch her skin, to wind her blonde hair around his hand as he forced her to submit, like halter-breaking a horse. All those fantasies where he stripped away her clothes to feast his eyes on her unblemished body. He imagined her flesh to be like porcelain, white and cool and smooth. Breasts firm with youth, unmarked by childbirth. Thighs, downy with golden hair and the woman part of her, unused by any other man before him.

He grinned then. His dreams were about to come true. Even better, he would repay Richard John a thousand-fold for the humiliation suffered in Guisborough court. Then he would only need to catch that damned boy, Valentine Rudd, and revenge would be complete. Oh, he was going to enjoy this. Every second.

"What...?" Margaret began.

He jerked her hair roughly. "Silence, girl." A vision of his wife, sour and unapproachable, swam into his mind, and his eyes stroked the girl's body again. Lust crawled groaning into his throat. With a start he realised his hand was trembling, the pistol muzzle almost grazing the skin from her nose. She was staring, mesmerised. Slowly, he uncocked it and pushed it into his belt. It was then she erupted. Struggling, she kicked and bit, scratching with fingers hooked into talons. Casually, he tightened his grip on her hair, twisting her head away so her attack was deflected. Only her feet, encased in soft shoes, hacked sideways at his shins, but his leather boots blunted her kicks.

He dragged her, spitting and cursing him, down the bank to the clearing where his gear lay next to the fallen tree. In the warm sunlight she looked even better. He turned her to face him, ignoring her hatred. Her voice shrill with terror, she screamed at him, but he slapped her hard with his free hand. Stunned, she gaped as a red welt appeared on her cheek. Twisting her hair so fiercely her features distorted, he took hold of the front of her dress. He had no time for buttons. With one wrench, he ripped the thin material down to her waist. She tried to cover herself. Angrily, he slapped her hands away. Her breasts were all he had imagined. Soft and rounded, nipples like rosebuds. Delicate. Vulnerable. She stood trembling, like a deer, awkward. Horrified, she stared into his eyes, reading the greed as they narrowed, switching back and forth, devouring her body.

Evil, her mind screamed, he is evil, evil. Her terror dismissed even the pain from his fingers threatening to uproot her tangled hair. Then his hand touched her. She recoiled, clamping her lips together to drown the scream that surged into her throat at the feel of his callused fingers. They cupped her breast, caressed then kneaded, more roughly as his excitement increased. She forced herself to look at his face. The leer, the dampening of his lips, his nostrils flaring as his breathing grew ragged.

"Take off your dress," he croaked, his hand furtively

touching the swelling at his crotch. Disgust curled her lip and he bridled, a hand snaking out to grab her waistband. Hanging tatters of cotton torn from her top hampered his first attempt. She shrank away, then jerked like a rag doll as he rived, teeth bared until the material shredded. With a grunt of triumph he ripped it down to her ankles. Her pantaloons split too, revealing a flash of thigh, and as he twisted her hair with his other hand she turned and he glimpsed the dark triangle of her womanhood. He lunged again, to grab at her pantaloons.

Defiance and pride evoked a desperate courage. Fear's grip loosened as her fists flailed at his chest and she spat in his face. She found her voice too, swooping from a tormented wail down to throaty husk as she sneered her contempt for him.

"You filth. You slime..."

He released her scalp then, slapping her to the ground. She sprawled on her back, dishevelled hair flung across her face. Frantically she brushed it aside.

"My father'll kill you!" she threatened as Hardiman towered over her, gloating, a hand already unfastening his belt buckle.

"And if he doesn't, I will," a voice promised.

Margaret's eyes shifted from Hardiman as he swung away. Beyond him stood Valentine Rudd. She had never been so glad to see anyone in her life. Even if it was him. But he was changed, no longer her father's lap dog. Older somehow, his face was set with anger, and absurdly the thought crossed her mind that he suddenly seemed handsome and tall. And it was the first time she had noticed he was broad in the shoulders and strong legged but gracefully narrow hipped. He almost looked like a squire's son, standing there in the black frockcoat, breeches and riding boots she had no doubt her father had given him.

Valentine's eyes flickered from the surprised Riding Officer to her for a second, then flickered back as though to spare her embarrassment. "Run," he said quietly. It was then she saw the bone handled crop in his hand, slapping his thigh in a mannerism she recognised as her father's. "Run, Margaret," he repeated softly.

She struggled to her knees, gathering the ruins of her dress as best she could. On her feet, hunched, protecting her naked breasts, she was confused. Without taking his eyes from Hardiman, Valentine gestured with the crop to the path.

As she began to hobble away, Hardiman snatched at the pistol butt protruding from his belt. He pulled it free, but before he could cock the hammer, Valentine was on him, his left hand grabbing Hardiman's wrist. He punched the Exciseman full in the face with his right hand, fingers still wrapped tight round the crop. The pistol fell useless to the ground and Valentine quickly kicked it spinning away into the grass.

Shouting, Hardiman lunged, fists flailing. Valentine took several blows then jabbed his assailant in the chest to drive him off. Staggering, Hardiman regained his balance and came on again. Valentine side-stepped and swiped the officer's head with the leather stock of the crop. Pivoting like a bullfighter, he faced the next attack. He feinted with the crop and when the Exciseman's hands rose to protect his head, Valentine kicked out viciously. The toe of his boot slammed into the other man's crotch. Hardiman grunted open mouthed, and as he folded, Valentine smashed the crop across the back of his neck.

Standing over him, Valentine realised he was panting and the short flurry of blows they had exchanged had quickly drained his strength. Now, the sight of Hardiman prostrate on the grass invoked an image of him wallowing in the waves on the beach that night. For a second Valentine regretted not killing him then. Now, teeth bared in anger, he kicked with all his strength. His boot drove under Hardiman's stomach, hooking him almost a foot into the air. His deadweight body smashed back into the ground like a dropped sack. He did not even grunt, no breath in his lungs. Valentine stooped, grabbed the Exciseman's shoulder and heaved him over. Blood was running from the corner of his mouth in frothy bubbles as air escaped his lips. His eyes opened slowly, unfocused, then slid shut.

Valentine hauled him up for another whipping with the crop but the moment he was released, Hardiman slumped back onto the ground. There seemed little point continuing to beat an unconscious man. Disgusted, Valentine kicked him once more then turned away.

Taking the path up out of the glen, Valentine passed only the black stallion. He strode along, casting both left and right for any sign of Margaret, but it was only when he neared Cliff House Wood that he heard whimpering. He splashed through the beck to find her crouched in the trees, hugging her knees, calves and feet muddy, her dress in tatters. Approaching, he shrugged off his coat then hung it gently round her shoulders.

Her eyes swung to him, wild, frightened, her mouth gaping, ready to scream. He backed off, hands open, palms up. "It's only me, Margaret. You're safe now." He spoke as if to a wild animal, fearful she would break and run.

"I... I..." She blinked rapidly, face contorted. Then her eyes seemed to return from some wild place haunted by her nightmares. She frowned. "Valentine?"

"Yes, it's me." It was the first time she had ever spoken his name. It sounded strange, not at all like when his mother or friends used it. He liked the way she said it. "Did he touch you?"

She glanced down at her breasts, protected by her arms and seemed surprised to see his coat round her shoulders. "His horrible hands and the way he leered at me... I feel dirty..."

Her voice trailed away and Valentine realised she was in shock. Her eyes roved back and forth across the ground, as though seeking reason in her confusion, then settled on him again.

"How? Where... I mean how did you...?"

"Your father asked me to find you and your mother said you'd gone walking in the woods. I heard you scream..."

She stiffened at the reminder of her ordeal, then repressed fears and hate and revulsion commenced battle in her mind. He read the emotions as they fought across her face before she finally relented and let go. Tears welled, then cut streaks down her face as she began to sob, thin shoulders wracking.

Sympathy stabbed Valentine's heart and he stepped forward, reaching. For an instant she went rigid, staring at him as though he was about to attack her, then she retreated into her shell of misery. Valentine bent to sit on the grass beside her, arm circling her shoulders.

"It's all right, Margaret. It's over now," he soothed, and she leaned into him, turning her head to nuzzle against his chest. How small and frail she is, he thought, soft and vulnerable. He had thought her tough and resilient, in command of her life, impetuous maybe and a manipulator with a whip for a tongue, but she was just a little girl really, lost and afraid and in need of protection. Once when his father had drunk too much, he had said that women have ten faces. When Valentine had asked what he meant, his father had shot him a piercing look, then turned to stare blindly into the night. You'll know soon enough, son.

As Margaret sobbed, he mumbled meaningless phrases meant to comfort but really only to let her know she was not alone. She cried her heart out, and he waited patiently. It seemed he had arrived before Hardiman had actually violated her, but she had endured a frightening assault and the threat of rape, an unenviable experience. That damned Exciseman. And what would Richard John do when he found out? If he blindly sought revenge, then the already closing authorities would trap him all the sooner. An angry man makes mistakes. What then? Valentine did not yet know enough to carry on the business.

He continued to squeeze Margaret's shoulder and offer solace. He had dreamed of holding her, but not this way. He would never have wished her this suffering just so he could hold her.

"It's over now," he whispered.

She pulled back to look at him. Eyes swimming with tears, he was struck again by their startling blue. Like the Caribbean, they seemed aware the subsiding storm was only the eye of the hurricane, wary of what was to follow. They moved from his face to the crop by his feet. "I wish I could have whipped him. God, how I would have hurt him." Her eyes narrowed and she squirmed, snuggling into the hollow of his shoulder, gazing off into the treetops. "I'd have flayed him. Every ounce of flesh from his bones."

Valentine saw she was pulling herself away from the abyss of madness then, using her anger to claw back. "You feel better now?"

"A little."

"We'd better get back. They'll be worrying." When she nodded, he climbed to his feet and lifted her gently, making sure his coat was still close about her shoulders to preserve her modesty.

"You're nice really, aren't you?" she said. When he didn't reply she continued, "When that man tore off my clothes, he stared at me like an object. I didn't feel human. But you took great pains not to look at me."

"I looked."

She studied him, but he quickly turned away to lead along the path. He took seven or eight strides, then halted abruptly. Almost stepping on his heels, she stumbled, then drew up. "What?"

Anguish and embarrassment teased his features before he brought them under control. "I looked, Margaret. You're the most beautiful thing I've ever seen."

She almost smiled then, but before Valentine saw she was not angry, he blushed and turned away again.

*   *   *

"You say Hardiman was unconscious when you left him?" Richard John queried, swinging round in his chair so his legs disappeared under the big desk. He was still commanding, even sitting, an almost visible aura of strength emanating from him. Even the room, his study, seemed to have soaked up his personality to emphasise his presence and the authority John managed to convey. But Valentine could see he was bristling with indignation, barely keeping his anger in check. His colour was high and he made a conscious attempt to keep his hands occupied. First fiddling with items on the desk, then filling his pipe which he had now abandoned in favour of a whisky glass.

"My men found nothing except where his horse had been tethered. Would that you had killed him on the spot." His face twisted into a malicious smile. "Although perhaps I'm glad you left me that privilege. I can see by your face that bothers you. Well, don't let it. I won't rush out and shoot him down like vermin, although he deserves no better. No, there's an old saying that revenge is a dish best eaten cold. And it's true. No, it'll be one dark night on a moor somewhere when he's poking his nose into my business, only it'll be the last place he ever pokes it. And I'll enjoy every moment of it."

He drained his glass and reached for the decanter. He glanced back at Valentine. "You want a drink? No? Well, you'd better sit down." He poured two fingers into his glass then held it up to the light. "Brandy or geneva, you can keep them. Nothing better than good Scotch whisky. It's rarer than honest men these days. Good job my customers don't agree." He eyed Valentine. "I want you out of that Exciseman's way. He'll be determined to catch you now, and he's clever enough to work out if you were protecting Margaret then you must be somewhere round this house. And here's the last place I want him sniffing. Besides, if he does have the gall to show up, I'm liable to lose my temper and kill him before I'm ready. No, I think it would be best if you went away for a while. Down the coast, maybe."

"I've relatives in Whitby," Valentine suggested.

A smile creased John's face. "Aye, Whitby would be fine." He thought a moment. "What relatives?"

"My father's cousin. Billy Rudd."

Richard John's smile widened. "Even better. Well, well, Billy Rudd. Can you leave tonight? I'll see you have a horse. Come and see me when you're ready to go."

EIGHT

The bay gelding was the one he had ridden to Hartlepool. Jacko the beachcomber had delivered him to the ferry after the horse's lameness had disappeared. Earlier, one of the grooms had brought him up to the main house and held him while Richard John said goodbye. Now, he snagged at the bit, shifting weight from hoof to hoof, side-stepping in a half circle each time he was allowed more than an inch of slack rein. In the saddle, Valentine melted into the animal's rhythm as he spoke to his father.

"Well son, you've got our Billy's address." Jackie Rudd said. "I took you to visit him when you were a little boy. He'll see you right." He reached to pat the gelding's arched neck, snatching his hand away as the bay swung snapping teeth. He laughed. "He'll give you a good ride. He's mean enough."

Sarah-Anne Rudd wore a worried frown. "Now don't you be getting yourself into mischief..."

Her husband shot her a warning look. "We've been through all that, love." He glanced up at his son and winked, the reason for Valentine's leaving kept from her. "Besides, he has his father's luck."

"What luck's that?" she inquired dryly.

"I got you, didn't I?"

She softened, casting her eyes down to hide her pleasure, before peering up again at her step-son. "Be careful on those moors."

Valentine sighed. "Mother. I'm only riding as far as Scaling tonight." He leaned down from the saddle and kissed her cheek when she rose onto tiptoe. "I'll be back before you know it."

He glanced at his father then shook hands. "I'll give your regards to Uncle Billy."

"Well, you heard your mother, son. Take care."

Valentine smiled. "I will." He touched heels to sleek flanks, raising a hand in farewell. The bay stepped out along the path in front of the cottages, toward the Ship Inn. He twisted in the saddle to see his father with his arm round Sarah-Anne, both waving. Then the path turned inland, widened for the coach that ran down from Brotton, a turning circle trodden behind the Ship Inn.

"Valentine! Valentine!"

He reined in the bay as he searched for the owner of the voice. Then he saw the black pony galloping flat out through Dove's farm, scattering chickens. Margaret was breathless when she hauled Blaze to a stop, her blonde hair blown into tangles round her face. He found it difficult to believe how clear-eyed and healthy she could look so soon after her ordeal.

"Father says you're going to Whitby." When he nodded she continued, "Because of me and what happened today." She glanced away, patting Blaze's neck as the pony's hooves scuffled on the track, his head jerking against the reins.

Valentine couldn't trust his voice. He had last seen her when he had led her into Cliff House. Only a few hours yet the thought of leaving for Whitby without seeing her one last time had been painful.

"I just wanted to say good-bye," she mumbled. "And to thank you. I'm sorry you're going." Her voice was soft and appealing, even a little shy, a stark contrast from the abrupt manner she had always previously used.

He smiled then. The ice was broken. "It'll only be for a few weeks, till things quieten down."

"When you come back, we can be friends," she offered. "I said some dreadful things about you. I'm sorry. You didn't deserve any of them."

"Well, not all of them," he grinned.

She laughed, then worry clouded her eyes. "You are coming back?"

"Of course."

She studied his face, searching for something. "Promise me you'll come back."

The longing in her voice made him laugh. "Try and keep me away."

Skilfully, she manoeuvred Blaze alongside the bay, then leaned across the gap to kiss his cheek. Before he could master his surprise at the feel of her lips, she had wheeled Blaze to canter away. Valentine watched until she disappeared up the bank toward Cliff House then clucked at the gelding. It needed no encouragement, turning up the road that wound round Huntcliff edge toward Brotton. Fleetingly, he looked back at Saltburn, then patted the bay's neck. "Come on, boy. You want to run, well now's your chance." Suddenly exuberant, he heeled the gelding and it stretched into a gallop.

*   *   *

Michael Cummins flicked the lash of his whip out over the team then with a deft jerk of the wrist cracked it inches from their ears. The two horses flinched and threw their weight into the traces. He glanced over his shoulder at his riding horse hitched to the cart's tailgate, then his attention was stolen by Freebrough Hill rising like an extinct volcano out of the moor behind them. He suppressed a shudder. It was said the earth had been moved by human hands, built as a burial mound hundreds of centuries ago. But Christ it was big. How many humans lay under it, for God's sake? It dominated the whole moor, making every mile within its sight creepy, especially when dusk was drawing in. As if the moors weren't spooky enough at night. An invisible hand made him shiver. With a curse at his own fear he swung back to look ahead at the road climbing past the Jolly Sailor Inn toward Scaling.

"Get a move on!" he shouted, wielding the whip again.

"What's the matter with you?" his wife enquired, snuggled inside a hooded cape which masked her face in shadow.

Cummins gurned his mouth in the half light. She looks like a cowled monk, he thought. He sometimes wondered whether someone had sent her to haunt him for the indiscretions of his youth. In this place, at this time of the day, it seemed certain.

"I asked you a question, Michael."

"And so you did," he answered. "There's nothing the matter."

"You're ruining those horses. You're too handy with that whip by far."

"We've got to make Scaling," he mumbled irritably. "The sooner they get us there the longer they'll have to rest before the journey tomorrow."

"There's plenty of time for..."

"Quiet!" Cummins' head was cocked, turning to the road behind them. Yes, there was something there...

"Don't you go interrupting me when I'm ..."

He was angry now. "I said shut up! Listen!"

"I can't hear anything."

"Nor will you if you keep talking."

Yes, hoofbeats. He squinted into the gloom. A rider, galloping, making good time. Although a boatman by profession, Cummins also prided himself on being a fair judge of horseflesh. Something about the animal's gait was familiar. If the light had been better, he could have placed it, he was sure. Perhaps his eyesight wasn't as good as it used to be. But no, they had accepted his word a few weeks ago when he identified old Richard John and that young lad in Guisborough Courthouse, hadn't they? He smiled, thinking of the gold guinea Richard John had given him when he passed on what Hardiman had said about wanting to murder the lad.

All he wanted now was some hot food and cold ale, and to leave Sybil at Egton. Her sister's time wasn't due for another week yet, so there was no great hurry. And he hated the farmhouse at Egton. And Sybil's sister. And her fat ruddy-cheeked husband. And farms. And tedious conversations about the breeding habits of pigs. And the poor condition of fields leased at an exorbitant rent. In fact he hated all of it, especially crossing this cursed moor at this time of day. He'd heard enough wittering about the expected baby every long evening throughout the winter when he'd been tied to the fireside while Sybil knitted booties and sweaters and scarves and hoods. The only good thing was he could leave Sybil at Egton to look after her sister's brood of breadsnappers, while he returned to Coatham, and with the weather improving, he could fish to his heart's content. And the codling would be running soon...

During his reverie, the rider had closed the gap. The regular drumming pattern of hoofbeats grew steadily louder behind them. Only a few yards, yet the light was so bad Cummins could not make out the horseman's face. Within seconds, the lather flecked gelding drew alongside the cart, and in that moment of being overtaken, Cummins' stare met the rider's. Then he was past, only the bay's tail streaming behind in the breeze to wish them farewell.

"Well, well," the boatman smirked, "and I wonder where he's going in such a hurry." He laughed then, slapping the reins over the team's rumps. "Get on with you, or you'll taste the whip!"

"Michael ..."

He flicked the lash, the crack of the leather startling in the quiet of dying day. "Silence woman, there's business to be done."

*   *   *

"Where are you off to, now?" Sybil demanded, flopping onto the lumpy bed, eyes wandering about the room.

Cummins placed her meagre baggage on the floor. He had

no interest in the decor, familiar with most of the rooms at the Bunch Of Grapes, having passed through Scaling hamlet many times. Even when not staying the night, the coaching inn was a regular call to slake his thirst or to warm his bones at the log fire. He called there often with Officer Hardiman too, in the capacity of carter when seized goods were being transferred from Marske to the King's warehouse at Whitby for transhipment to London. Now, he was anxious to go downstairs.

"You make yourself comfortable. I'll away down and see if there's any hot food."

"You mean you want to swill ale," she accused.

"Maybe a tankard or two."

She nodded, resigned. "Not overmuch. I know what you're like when you start."

Downstairs, Cummins' gaze swept the bar. Three or four drinkers clustered at the serving counter, stoking pipes and discussing the merits of Suffolk sheep compared to Leicesters. Almost as interesting as pig-breeding. When the landlord saw him, he left the group and began to pull a pint of best bitter. Cummins stepped round the farmers to an empty stretch of bar.

"The lady wife settled in?" the landlord asked, concentration focused on easing the pump so the head on the beer was perfect.

Cummins grunted. "As ever, Daniel. Any grub on the go?"

The pewter tankard was pushed carefully toward him. "Some broth I think. And fresh bread and cheese."

"Gamekeeper's broth?"

"Aye, but the gamekeeper doesn't know about this pan of venison and rabbit."

Cummins smiled. "Taste all the better for it too, I don't doubt. Can you send some up to the wife? I'll have mine down here." He sank a long draught of ale, then wiped his mouth with the back of his hand. "Ah, Daniel, you keep a good cellar."

"An even better one when the king's men aren't about," Daniel quipped, referring to Hardiman who he hated.

The boatman laughed, glancing at the other drinkers. "Quiet in here tonight. No coaches?"

Daniel consulted the clock on the wall behind the bar. "Not due for another hour yet."

"Wonder if there's many passengers?" Cummins mused. "You could do with the trade at this time of year."

"I won't argue with that," the landlord conceded. "Mind you, there's already another guest apart from yourself and the wife."

"Yes, I saw a bay gelding in the stable. Somebody travelling on business, I suppose."

Daniel shook his head. "A young lad."

"Wonder where he's bound."

The landlord eyed the boatman. "Whitby. At least he asked how many miles it was."

"Suppose he's off to visit relatives, then."

"Dunno, didn't say. Just ordered something to eat, asked how far, then went off to bed. Didn't even wet his whistle." Daniel grunted. "Customers like that I don't need."

Cummins laughed, drained his tankard and pushed it back across the bar. "Think I've got time for another?"

The landlord strolled down the bar to where a door stood open into the kitchen. "Two bowls of broth, love, and bread and cheese!" He returned and with a wink began to pull a pint. "I should say so." He placed the foaming tankard on the counter then reached for another and stood it on the bartop. "If you offered, I might join you." He grinned. "I think you owe me one."

"Eh?" Cummins frowned.

Daniel grinned. "A pint of ale. Cheap at the price for picking my brains, don't you think?"

*   *   *

Valentine was sweating. Even the breeze generated by the bay's canter was not enough to cool the spring morning. A full breakfast inside him, Valentine slouched in the saddle and gave the gelding its head. Scaling was a good three or four miles behind and he spent his time examining the changing land as he rode. The road topped out on ridges then it would abruptly dip and twist through hollows where fresh streams scoured. A light frost had melted away to reveal the heather's royal purple, carpeting miles of moor inland to the south on his right. In the north, green fields bordered the coast along by Runswick and Kettleness, while peeking through a cluster of trees was Ugthorpe mill, sails slowly groaning as they turned in the slack breeze. Here the highway ran straight, climbing steadily for almost half a mile before swinging downward in a long sweep and then curving away up another hill to Aislaby Moor Top. He passed the road to Egton Bridge, a bare limbed tree a stark marker.

In contrast, on his left lay a long tract of rich green timber, Hutton Mulgrave Wood melting into Skelder Plantation where pines retained year round coats. A farmhouse nestled in a clearing, geese and chickens squabbling over the morning feedcorn. The farmer's wife paused when she heard hoofbeats and peered toward the road, waving good-naturedly. The bay stumbled, composure lost for a moment before regaining his stride. Then they were at the moor top. Valentine reined in, bringing the gelding to a standstill. While the horse blew, ribs heaving, shaking out his mane and stamping away cramp's gnarled fingers, Valentine stared at the view spread below.

The land fell away from his feet, rolling down in a puckered blanket of green fields scored by the track of the highway swooping and curving toward the coastline. Dwellings were scattered across the land, smoke curling from kitchen chimneys while cattle grazed in the meadows, a lone shepherd working his sheep toward a wattle pen. His command whistles, high then low, sharp and soothing, carried up to Valentine who listened with a smile. Of more interest, beyond the circling collie, lay his journey's end.

Whitby straddled the gash in the coast which was the mouth of the River Esk. On the near side were few buildings, but facing him the cliff was dominated by the vast ruin of the abbey. Stripped and plundered since Henry VIII dissolved the monasteries in the 1500s, yet almost three quarters of the walls still stood, tall, black and gaunt against the sky. Sunlight shone through empty window casements, sculpted in elegant arches. Massive buttressed walls of dressed masonry looked powerful enough to withstand the vagaries of the weather and the subtle siege of time. There could be few more fitting monuments to man's faith and perseverance. The abbey's tower was almost an older relation to the smaller one of St Mary's Church, also standing on the cliff top. As Valentine watched, patches of cloud and sunshine chased each other over abbey and church, illuminating briefly the ragged ranks of sandstone grave markers. Wind scoured up from the beach over the black rocks of the cliff to rake the long churchyard grass, its salty tang calling perhaps to the bones of the many mariners anchored below the soil. Breezy fingers traced their fading names on the pockmarked headstones. They were the lucky ones, come home to die. Whitby lived on the sea, and the sea lived on Whitby. The German Ocean, also known as the Widow Maker, always levied toll for gathering the bounty of her waters.

Valentine found the abbey oppressive, yet somehow reassuring. The builders' faith in their God he could not understand, but he appreciated their craftsmanship. He stared at the ruin, then let his gaze fall to the shamble of smoke-smeared cottages clinging to the Cliff. Red pantile roofs overlapping, almost leaning on each other, they seemed to overhang from the top of the cliff to the bottom. Somewhere among them lived his Uncle Billy. Valentine patted the letter he carried inside his coat, then touched his heels to the bay. Steel-shod hooves clattered on the road as the gelding lurched from a walk into a trot then fell into the easy rhythm of a mile-eating canter. He would be there by dinner time.

*   *   *

Whitby harbour was divided in two by a draw bridge which could be raised when shipping demanded access. As Valentine Rudd walked the gelding across the hollow planking he glanced downstream at the fishing boats berthed shoulder to shoulder along the staithe. Crews were sorting morning catches on blood-slippy decks among a confusion of crab pots, nets and cables. Gutted fish were packed into creels, while overhead, herring gulls swirled, screaming and mewing as they darted in to steal offal.

On his right, the upper harbour seemed peaceful, the whaling fleet moored at dolphins. Those in need of physical repair had already visited dry dock during the winter, now tended by a flotilla of boats ferrying equipment for the coming season at the Greenland Fishery. Topmasts were being hoisted on one, while on another shouts and curses urged construction of a web of rigging. One vessel stood in the dock, men scurrying about her keel. The clang of shipwrights' hammers echoed from the harbour walls and the smell of hot tar drifted downstream as caulkers worked their irons into her seams. In mid-stream a brawny seaman called "Look alive, there!" gaffing a trailing hawser by the mainchains of a whaler which carried the name *Henrietta* gilded across her transom. The seaman stood in the prow of a longboat piled high with coils of new cable, hemp white in the sun. Before Valentine's gelding stepped from the drawbridge, the seaman had already secured his boat fore and aft and was bellowing for a hoist from the deck windlass.

"Here, young fellow! Watch where you're going!"

An indignant man shook a fist at Valentine. Expensively

dressed, probably a merchant or shipowner, he was shielding his wife who was pressed against the wall. Valentine realised she was frightened of the horse and casually twisted his wrist. The gelding obeyed immediately, veering round the couple. Valentine gave a half smile, touching his hat brim in apology.

The first street, Sandgate, was little more than a tight alley. Church Street lay a few yards on. He turned the bay's head into the narrow thoroughfare, clogged with pedestrians and carts unloading merchandise onto the cobbles. The shops stood barely yards apart and Valentine kept the bay to a walk as people squeezed out of his path, plodding on past the tollbooth at the top of the market square. The street began to curve toward the foot of the 199 church stairs that ascended to the clifftop. The crowd thinned, then he saw it.

The whitewashed cottage was tiny, a whaling harpoon bracketed to the wall by the door. Valentine halted the bay and leaned down from the saddle. The rusted metal was scaly, flaking at his touch. He had heard harpoon steel was so well-tempered it was pliable enough to be rebeaten into shape after being bent. Under his stare this one seemed to have lost its magic and Valentine quelled his disappointment. He dropped the dead metal scales then banged on the door. It was opened by a youth his own age, dressed in a stained fishing smock and canvas trousers tucked into seaboots. He took a look at Valentine's dark broadcloth suit and the fine gelding. He sniffed disdainfully.

"Now then. What'd you be wanting here?"

Valentine ignored the glower. "I'm looking for Billy Rudd."

"What for?"

Valentine's temper began to rise. "What's it to you? Now, does he live here or not?" he demanded, tapping his crop against his leather boots. It was a trick he had learned from Richard John.

"Who wants him?" the youth asked, this time less impudent. Before Valentine could answer, the youth's glare crumpled as he was shouldered aside by an older man, obviously his father. Thick necked and stocky, they guarded the cottage door like two bulldogs.

"Billy Rudd?"

"Aye, that's me," the man admitted.

Valentine smiled then. "Your cousin Jackie is my father."

Billy's face was blank for a moment as he stared up at the well-dressed young man on the horse, then his jaw dropped. "Then you'll be Valentine. Well, I never." He grinned then, gesturing a foot or two above the ground. "I haven't seen you since you were that high. Well, get down, son, and come in."

Valentine dismounted and pulled the reins forward over the bay's head to act as a halter. "What do I do with my horse?"

Billy waved a hand. "Jonathan here'll take care of him. He can go in the yard for the time being." He eyed the carpetbag tied behind the saddle cantle, then grinned. "Better bring that in. Looks like you didn't just call for tea."

Jonathan glowered at being given orders in front of the stranger but obeyed as his father wrapped a strong arm about Valentine's shoulders and led him inside. A driftwood fire smoked in the grate, a kettle steaming next to a pan of bubbling stew. A woman stood guard over them, wooden spoon in her hand. Billy called to her and she turned to face the door. Life had scored deep lines either side of her mouth, hardening her features into permanent discontent. But her eyes were bright as buttons beneath her bonnet.

"Who's this, then?" she asked.

Valentine smiled at her as Billy introduced him.

"So if he's your cousin Jackie's son, what does that make him?"

Billy pursed his lips. "I don't rightly know. Something like a nephew once removed, I should think." He shrugged the matter aside. "That's not important. He's family, and that's all that counts."

"Surely," she agreed. "Sit yourself down. Have you eaten? I'm about to put the dinner out."

"I'd be honoured to eat with you," Valentine flattered, hopeful it would soften her demeanour. It worked. She smiled, then caught herself and motioned to a chair.

"Only stew, but it's filling."

"I'm sure it will be delicious. Thank you."

She looked pointedly at Jonathan. "He may be a Rudd, but he has good manners. More than some."

Valentine noted the by-play as he sat down, eyes roving the room. It reminded him very much of his home in Saltburn. Everything well worn, but carefully tended and scrupulously clean. A comfortable, snug room. The mantelpiece bore knick-knacks probably gathered through a lifetime. Marks of the sea were everywhere. Carved models of fully rigged ships, even one in a bottle, and scrimshaw – whale's teeth etched with evocative scenes of the Greenland Fishery. He leaned forward from his chair to study a fine example of patience and skill.

Billy noticed his curiosity. He reached for the tooth then passed it to Valentine. "My father, Bob Rudd carved that. He was a harpooner in the trade. That one on the wall outside was his, from his last season. Frostbite ruined his livelihood. The ship's surgeon had to chop three fingers off his right hand." He grimaced. "It was his throwing hand. He never went to the Greenland Sea again. They say he was one of the best. Could throw near as far as Cap'n Scoresby." He faded into silence, briefly examining the scrimshaw when Valentine handed it back before replacing it on the mantelpiece.

"I saw them outfitting the whalers as I came over the bridge," Valentine commented.

Billy broke into a smile. "Aye, they'll soon be off." He nodded at his son. "Our Jonathan's been apprenticed on *Northern Star* under Cap'n Falton."

"Do you sail with them?"

Billy shook his head. "No, I've got enough here to keep me busy. I've a fishing sloop called *Speedwell*. She's the second I've had of that name. I lost the first when that pirate John Paul Jones captured her." His eyes glazed for a moment, locked in the past, then he smiled again. "If our Jonathan can make a few bob on *Northern Star* – she's supposed to be lucky ship – then he'll have a nest egg. When he's back he can fish with me. Let's hope she is lucky. Falton is a good man. He knows his business. Our Jonathan should do all right there."

"It sounds exciting," Valentine commented. "I almost wish I was going with you," he added, glancing at his young relative. Jonathan snorted and looked away.

"Here. Eat it while it's hot." Billy's wife offered Valentine a bowl of steaming stew. He accepted it gratefully. They were all quiet for some minutes while they ate, Billy finishing first. He stoked his pipe with fresh tobacco then patiently waited until the plates were clean. He smiled when Valentine complimented the lady of the house on the meal, then lit his pipe with a taper from the fire and settled back, eyeing the young visitor speculatively.

"Well now, what brings you to Whitby?"

"Like my father and you, I'm a fisherman." He noted Billy's glance at his suit. "Or I was. Now I work for Richard John." He paused, studying Billy's bland expression. "I know you don't need any explanation about that. We'll talk about that later. As how I come to be here, well, it's a long story..."

"I'm listening."

Valentine took a deep breath then launched into an account of his adventures under Richard John's wing, finishing with Hardiman's murder threat and Margaret's near rape in the woods. Nobody interrupted to ask questions. Silent, he glanced round the three attentive faces. Judging from his expression, even Jonathan seemed to admit a grudging respect,

"You only work for Richard John, or is there more to it?"

The question surprised Valentine as he caught a brief glint in Billy's eyes.

"It's not so simple."

Billy grunted. "It never is. Well?"

"I've been living in his house since I was wounded on the beach that night. And, his daughter, well... What I mean is..."

Billy smiled. "So, he's taken you into his house and you're courting his daughter and he knows. He's also given you expensive clothes and a horse and sent you here for a while until that Riding Officer, Hardiman, has cooled down a bit."

Valentine nodded. "That's about it."

Billy sniffed and sucked at his dead pipe. "Well, there's more to it than just working for Richard John, isn't there?" When Valentine did not answer, Billy nodded. "I thought as much." He glanced at his wife. "You said you had some shops to visit?" The tone of his voice brought her from her chair. "Jonathan, you'll have to buy feed for the lad's horse." He dipped into a pocket and produced some coins.

"I've money to take care of the gelding," Valentine interrupted.

"You can owe me. Jonathan, the farrier at the Dragon Yard livery will sell you a bale of hay." He waited until his wife and son left the cottage, using the time to carefully retamp his pipe. When they had gone, he peered questioningly at Valentine who slipped a hand inside his jacket and produced the letter.

Billy stood up to rummage on the mantelpiece. He found a small case, opened it and hooked the arms of a pair of spectacles over his ears, before seeking a knife to attack the envelope.

"Only wear 'em for reading, mind," he blustered, embarrassed. "I'm all right with books, but handwriting is hard sometimes."

Valentine smiled sympathetically, then watched Billy struggle through the letter, mouthing words and occasionally holding the parchment at arm's length before drawing it slowly toward his nose as he strained to focus on difficult words. He realised Billy must be reading it through twice. Apparently, this branch of the Rudds took less pains in teaching their children to read and write. Once more he appreciated his step-mother's patience.

"So Richard John will not be here at the next run on..." he peered at the letter, "Wednesday next. He says I am to regard you as having his authority." He looked at Valentine with a wary eye. "You were right when you said it was complicated. Here I am, suddenly taking orders from a lad no older than my own son."

Valentine waved a dismissive hand. "You know what to do and when to do it. The letter only means if things go wrong..."

"Is he expecting them to? Doesn't he trust me? I've handled his goods for nigh on eight years now," he added indignantly.

"He trusts you, Uncle Billy," Valentine reassured, for the first time referring to their family relationship. "You're a Rudd. So am I. Rudds are trustworthy. Like you said yourself, things aren't as simple as they used to be. Runs have been going wrong all up and down the coast. The Revenue have decided to come down hard and make an example. They've picked Richard John. That's why he won't be here. He has other matters to attend to." He examined Billy's face as he absently tapped the letter against his knee.

"You'd better burn it."

"Eh?" Billy's eyes focused. "What am I thinking of?" He leaned forward and flipped the envelope onto the driftwood fire. The edges charred before it burst into flames. "Things have been going wrong, eh? Well, it never was the surest of livings. Or the safest."

Valentine wondered then whether he should reveal Richard John's predictions for the contraband trade; how this was the beginning of the end, then decided against it. The knowledge could possibly cloud his uncle's judgement at a crucial moment. Besides, it may have just been an old man's drunken ramblings.

The day after the revelations, Richard John had continued as if nothing had changed. He wondered whether John even remembered the conversation.

"Uncle Billy. Richard John trusts me and he trusts you. Few other people. There are spies and informers everywhere. It was a Revenue boatman who gave us the warning Hardiman is out to murder me. If their men are telling us, how many of our men are informing to them?"

The older man's eyes turned steely, voice indignant. "You're accusing one of my men of being an informer? Never. I picked every man myself. And they know what I'd do to them if they betrayed me."

Valentine made a calming gesture. "I'm not saying there's a spy. I'm only saying it's possible. You may have picked the best men in Whitby, but circumstances could force one of them to inform, no matter how much he fears you or hates to do it."

Billy studied his young relative. "I trust their sense of loyalty to Mr John and to me."

"Loyalties can be forgotten when families are in trouble."

"Perhaps you're right."

Valentine stared into the fire at the curled ashes of the letter. "Let's hope I'm wrong."

NINE

Hardiman thrust the spade into the earth, then leaned back to stretch the aches from his muscles and wipe a soiled handkerchief across his face. He confessed he was seriously out of condition. Catching his breath, he surveyed the wasteland of his vegetable garden. After the last cabbages had been cut, the land had lain fallow through the rest of winter. He had promised to devote some time to it, but then he always did. The result was his potatoes should have been planted weeks since, pushing up above ground by now, but instead, well over half the garden remained undug, coated with horse manure and compost in hope the land would glean some succour before being put to use.

He tucked the handkerchief back in his pocket, then spat on his hands. If he didn't get it done now, then he never would. He grabbed the spade, and heaved the earth over, chopping it a few times to help the weather break it up. It wasn't so bad after all. Physical labour somehow felt right, working with nature. Soil under his fingernails and the aroma of rotting manure in his nostrils. It was the only thing that felt right about his life at that moment. The rest was a mess. Since the fiasco in court, nothing had gone smoothly. And then that arrogant young bastard interrupting him in the woods when he was about to... God, to think he had got so close to tasting her young flesh! Angrily, he thrust the spade back into the ground, narrowly missing his foot. He swore aloud.

"Good-day."

Hardiman looked up. Cummins, the boatman was leaning on the fence, a grin revealing uneven teeth. Hardiman glared at him.

"You'll be smiling too in a minute," Cummins said.

"That would take a miracle."

Cummins raised his eyebrows. "I might be delivering one."

"Will it turn over this garden, plant my potatoes and have them sprout overnight?"

"For a guinea, I'll tell you."

Hardiman snorted. "For a guinea I need two miracles."

"You'll pay when you know." Cummins was serious now.

"I'll be the judge of that. Well, get on with it. I haven't all day." He planted the spade and stood with hands on hips, his mouth turned down by impatience.

"Valentine Rudd."

Hardiman's gaze revealed nothing. "What of him?"

"I saw him myself at the Bunch of Grapes at Scaling, the day afore yesterday. Rudd asked the landlord how far it was to Whitby."

"Means nothing." Hardiman pursed his lips. "If you've come back, so could he."

The boatman shook his head. "I've friends in Saltburn. Nobody has seen him. Word is he's laying low. And besides, he was riding a bay gelding."

"He can't afford a horse."

"I know. He can't afford a fine suit either, but he was wearing one. I fancy all three belong to Richard John. The horse, the suit and the boy." He was quiet then, watching the Riding Officer's face.

Hardiman was deep in thought. Rudd was seen going to Whitby, and he had asked how far, which meant he'd never been there before. So why should he go now? If Richard John had lent him a horse, there was more than a chance the reason was business. Well, if Rudd had friends in Whitby, so did he. Rudd shouldn't be that hard to find. Especially if there was business in the wind. Hardiman uprooted his spade and strode toward the house. "Wait by the back door," he said over his shoulder as he stood the spade against the wall and entered the house.

When he emerged he was carrying an overnight bag, coat and hat in the other hand. He dropped the carryall on the step and pressed a gold coin into the boatman's hand. "You're right, you earned it." As Cummins touched his cap in thanks, Hardiman's wife appeared in the doorway behind him.

"Look at you! Muddy bootprints all over my scullery floor. Have you no sense?" She spied his bag. "Where are you off to now? Scarcely a word for three days, ready to bite the children's heads off every time you see them, and suddenly you're off with no thought of explanation."

Hardiman stood with his back to her during the tirade, staring into the distance. Then he turned slowly, thunder in his eyes. His voice was chilling. "Be quiet, woman. I'm doing my job."

"Dad! Dad!" a voice screeched as a child appeared beside his wife. About eight years old, he was a raggedly dressed urchin, barefoot, unkempt hair hanging in his eyes. He leaned close to his mother's skirts and she placed a protective arm about him.

"Don't bother your father now, Jamie," she shushed.

He looked up at her, puzzled. "There's a man at the front door wants Dad. Says it's ur-ur-ur..."

"Urgent," Cummins supplied.

Hardiman shot him a scathing glance. "That right, son?" When the boy nodded, he continued: "Tell him to come round the back. I've got my muddy boots on and I don't want to tread it through the house." He glanced at his wife who smiled primly. The boy released her skirts and ran off through the kitchen. "What now?" Hardiman wondered aloud, turning to face the back gate where his son appeared a few seconds later. A hatless man followed him, wearing a pigtail that bounced on the shoulder of his striped jersey. Wide canvas trousers flapped above buckled shoes. The newcomer touched his finger to his forehead in a loose salute.

"Officer Hardiman?" He received a curt nod. "Captain's compliments, sir, and this despatch." He offered a waterproof canvas bag to Hardiman who accepted it then turned away to walk along the garden path as he broke the wax seals. He scanned the document then reread it slowly. Satisfied, he returned to the house where wife, son, boatman and sailor all watched him.

"Cummins, you can do me a service. Roust out the Dragoons and ride with them to the Bay Hotel at Runswick. Take my horse with you. I'll be aboard *Ferret*. When you get there, keep a sharp lookout and when you see her in the bay meet me at the slipway. Understand?"

A glint appeared in Cummins' eye. "The usual rate?"

Hardiman gave a half smile. "And a bonus if the matter we spoke about earlier proves true. Right, get on with you." As the boatman left, the Riding Officer swung toward the sailor. "My compliments to your Captain and I'll be with you directly."

The man's mouth narrowed. "Begging your pardon, sir, but wind and tide will only favour us for the next half hour."

"I said directly," Hardiman snapped.

"Aye aye, sir."

Hardiman watched until the sailor was out of the gate, then turned to his wife. "I should be back in a few days."

"You're going to Runswick Bay? That's not your area. It belongs to the Whitby officer."

"It's Whitby I'm going to. The officer there needs help. And if things turn out the way I expect, then my problems could be solved. I need a good arrest to set the record straight."

"Richard John, isn't it?" she asked, worry clouding her eyes.

He nodded. "Yes, him. But more besides." He kissed her cheek dutifully. A hand tugged at his breeches and he smiled down at his son. He reached down and scooped him up to kiss his grubby face.

"Where are you going, Dad?" Jamie asked.

Hardiman smiled wryly. "Daddy's going a-hunting."

*   *   *

Hardiman stood on *Ferret's* tiny quarterdeck as she ploughed south-east across the surge of the flowing tide. A landsman, he shifted his feet awkwardly as she heeled, her fore and aft sails billowing with wind. Casually, he slid his hands behind his back to grip the taffrail, legs spread wide to absorb the corkscrew motion of the cutter as she crested waves which rushed underneath to lift her transom before dropping it into the following sea. Queasy, he looked away from the rolling German Ocean and stared landward at rugged cliffs fringing the skyline. He recognised nothing, hoping the journey would end before he embarrassed himself.

"Full and bye!" the helmsman called.

"Steady as she goes," the mate cautioned, then leaned forward to speak to James Major. "We've cleared Lingrow Knock, sir. When we've weathered the Cobble dump we can stand in."

Lt-Commander James Major stood straight as a flagpole and almost as slender, hands clasped behind his waist as he strolled the narrow quarterdeck. Expressionless, he maintained a controlled facade to subordinates. "Very well, Mr Dykes. Don't forget the rock ledges run about five cables eastward from the dump. Swing well clear. We'll be anchoring for the night. When she's squared away, have a boat lowered to take Mr Hardiman ashore. Send a runner below when you're ready. Carry on." He glanced at his guest and gestured to the companion ladder. Hardiman pushed away from the rail, staggering a little, unable to emulate the officer's anticipation of the cutter's rolls.

The stern cabin under the quarterdeck was barely large enough to contain a cot, desk and chair, beams a scant five feet from the deck. Daylight peeped through a skylight hatch, voices from the deck carrying below. Hardiman wondered how many times Major had heard comments not meant for his ears. Hardiman accepted a glass of brandy, taking the chair. The captain sat on the cot, sipped his own drink then pursed his lips.

"Rackam at Whitby said he had solid information. When we anchor, I'll set the men to tasks as though we're undertaking running repairs. That'll stop the locals getting too nosey for a couple of days. You can get a message to me by rider. The only other safe anchorage is at Sandsend and that's too close. It can be seen plainly from Whitby with a glass. We don't want the *Ferret* to scatter the chickens before the run starts." He smiled at his own joke, then his smile died. "You think *Morgan Butler* will be involved?"

Hardiman smothered a cough caused by the raw brandy. "It's certain to be. We can't prove it yet, but we're sure *Morgan Butler* is owned by Richard John, and of every ten runs on this coast, his hand is in eight." He took another sip. "If the information is right, it all points toward him. I think you want Captain Josiah Brown as badly as I want Richard John. The question is, how much are you prepared to lose to get him?"

"Enough." Major's eyes shone. "More brandy?"

Hardiman matched the other's grin. "A man after my own heart."

*   *   *

Whitby's Riding Officer, James Rackam was a rake of a man, hollow eyed, his haggard face constantly darkened by shaving blue. Aged thirty-six, his once raven hair was streaked with grey, a fact that always amazed him when confronted by his own image in a mirror. Sleepless nights while boots rattled on the cobbles outside his cottage had scored deep lines either side of a mouth set in a permanent downturn. Dour, the Scots called it, Hardiman thought, and that was the best damned word for it too. Dressed in a black frockcoat, Rackam looked like an undertaker. Only shiny black riding boots dispelled the image, and the way he sat his horse, arrogant like a lord of the manor. No, not a likeable man, and such a miserable bastard, Hardiman thought, then laughed under his breath. He wasn't exactly happy himself.

Rackam dug his spurs into the grey, glancing sideways. "Not far. The cottage stands short of West Cliff, near the Mulgrave Castle Inn on Upgang." His mount leapt ahead into the evening gloom.

Hardiman heeled his own black to catch up. When the longboat from the *Ferret* had put him ashore, Cummins had been there, holding the head of his horse, while Rackam impatiently stalked up and down Runswick sands. Barely had Hardiman waded through the breaking surf than Rackam had pulled him to one side and explained they had a call to make and to leave the Dragoons at Runswick. After some argument he had agreed to let Cummins accompany them in case a messenger was needed to bring the soldiers. Rackam had led them along farm tracks to avoid the villagers in Lythe and Sandsend passing on information. Talking as they rode, it became clear Rackam had only asked for extra Dragoons. The Comptroller, however, had ordered Hardiman's presence when it appeared the projected run was one of Richard John's. Conversation also revealed Rackam was none too happy about Hardiman's presence. But then, the Marske officer reflected, the long faced misery probably wished to secure all the glory for himself. For once, Hardiman was glad of the Comptroller's decision. Given the possibility of laying hands on Richard John, and more specifically Valentine Rudd, he could certainly endure Rackam.

Ahead, Rackam slowed his horse to a walk. Hardiman reined in and signalled Cummins to slow. Almost dark, the moon rose to lay a silver path across the sea on their left as they moved down the headland toward the cliff edge. Off to the right lay a sprawl of well lit buildings, smoke curling from four chimneys. Closer stood a tumbledown cottage, pantiles awry, walls bellied by subsidence as the low cliff was slowly devoured by the German Ocean. The whitewash was flaked and the window frames almost naked of paint. Approaching from the gable end, Hardiman's eyes strayed to the rear of the cottage where pigsties and a stable looked in equally poor repair.

"Houseproud, isn't he?" Hardiman commented. "How many live here?"

"The informant, his wife and four children."

"Good God, how does he feed them?" Hardiman speculated aloud.

Rackam smiled thinly. "Like the rest, by evading the King's dues."

"Will he run?" When Rackam shrugged, Hardiman gestured to Cummins. "Tie your horse here and go round the back. We'll give you two minutes." The boatman dismounted and faded into the shadows. Hardiman wasted time by glancing at the surrounding land, familiarising himself. "He informed before?"

"A hint now and again. Sometimes right, sometimes wrong."

"What makes you believe him this time?"

Rackam's met Hardiman's. "It felt right. I can smell it when they're lying. He's greedy. Whatever he gets for unloading the luggers, it isn't enough, otherwise he wouldn't risk talking to me."

Hardiman nodded, peering toward the outbuildings. No sign of Cummins. He jerked his head. They trotted the horses to the door where Rackam swung down from the saddle. The handle of his crop clattered on the peeling wood. He waited for a bare ten seconds then rapped again. When there was still no reply he half turned to speak, then pasted on a smile as the door cracked open. A woman's face, hair hidden by a bonnet, peeped out, obviously frightened.

"Ah, Mrs Gooch. Is your husband at home?"

She shook her head too quickly, too nervously.

Rackam's smile never faltered. His hand shot out to grab the edge of the door only inches from her face while his riding boot shot forward into the gap. "Well, we'll just have to see for ourselves, won't we?"

"You can't come in!" she shrieked, head turned so anyone inside would hear. Rackam held the door ajar, grinning at Hardiman. "If you would be so kind." He jerked his head at the side of the cottage.

There was a scuffling in the darkness at the rear. Hardiman edged his mount toward an aisle between pigsties. Two men were struggling. One fell to his knees, grunting with pain, before being hauled upright and pinned against a wall. Just then, the rear door of the cottage opened. Rackam emerged, holding a lantern aloft.

"A little trouble out here?" he inquired mildly.

"All taken care of," Cummins answered hoarsely.

"Good. Shall we inspect the stable?" As he moved down the path Mrs Gooch appeared in the doorway, anxious.

"Jack, are you all right?"

Her husband mumbled. Rackam looked back over his shoulder. "Just a little talk, Mrs Gooch. Nothing to worry about." He gestured to the boatman. "Get him into the stable."

Inside, Rackam dropped the cross batten to seal the door, then hung the lantern on a peg to free both his hands. Jack Gooch was a small, wiry man, unshaven, lank hair hanging to his shoulders. His eyes were like those of a trapped animal as he backed against the stall timbers. On the other side, a sway-backed shire horse snickered, hooves shuffling.

"Gooch." Rackam said wearily. "I don't think you told me everything the other day."

The informer shook his head, eyeing the crop. "There's nothing more, Mr Rackam. I told you all I know." He failed to portray an honest expression, hands palm upward. "I gave you a good guinea's worth."

The King's man sighed, slumping defeated shoulders. "I'm trying to be polite, Jack. You know me, I'm not a vicious man. I believe you told me everything. However... this is Officer Hardiman who has ridden a long way and his temper is a little shorter than mine." He feigned regret. "Now, Mr Hardiman thinks you should have told me more, but I said there was no more. Am I right?"

Gooch nodded. "Yes, Mr Rackam."

"You sure?"

"Oh yes. I wouldn't lie to you." His confidence was growing. "Even if I knew any more, I couldn't tell you. It would be more than my life's worth."

Rackam shook his head again, slowly, regretfully. "Jack, I'm a fair man. But I'm not stupid. You must have been told when you'll be needed for the business."

"I can't tell you that."

"Can't or won't?"

Gooch grimaced. "I know you been fair with me, but they'll kill me if I tell you..."

Hardiman stepped forward into the light, fists bunched.

Rackam reached a restraining hand to Hardiman's shoulder. "No need for that..."

The Marske officer snarled. "Yes, there is. I'm sick of these people. I've heard it all too many times – *turn your face to the wall while the gentlemen ride by. What you don't know can't hurt you* – Well there are none of them gentlemen, they're all scum. They call themselves 'Free-traders' but they're thieves, rogues and murderers." He shrugged away Rackam's hand then grabbed Gooch's shirt and hauled him up onto tip-toe. "Tell us what you know, Gooch, and quickly, or your wife'll be laying you out in the morning." He glared into the informer's face. "My horse gets edgy when there's slime like you under his hooves. If I stabled him here for the night with you, he'd likely as mash you to pulp by morning. And nobody'd be any the wiser."

"That'd be murder," Gooch choked, his hand grabbing to free his throat where the Riding Officer's hands were closing like a vice.

Hardiman slapped his hand away and tightened his grip. "Who'd prove it? A horse who trampled you to death by accident could hardly be held responsible." He choked off a laugh. "Remember Gooch, you've a wife and a bunch of rug-rats to feed. Now tell us what you know." He stared into the informer's eyes, then slowly pulled a fist back, lantern light glinting on his white knuckles.

Rackam caught his arm. "There's no need for that. You'd best go outside for the time being. I'll question Mr Gooch." Reluctantly, Hardiman released his grip, flicking his hands away from him as though to rid them of any taint from the informer's clothes. He glared at him once more in unspoken promise then turned for the door. He lifted the batten then abruptly spun round, voice harsh, full of menace. "Five minutes, that's all you've got, then I'll be back. Think about it." He swung open the stable door, and before it closed behind him he could hear Rackam's voice, soothing now.

"...I warned you about Officer Hardiman. He's a hard man and he means what he says. I've heard he broke all the fingers of a man who refused to help him. Now, be reasonable about this. He's right, you've got your wife and children to think about..."

Outside, Hardiman stood in the dark, sucking down sea air. He stared at the moon-silvered ocean, listening to the booming of the breakers on the beach a hundred yards away. Somewhere out there was *Morgan Butler*, holds stuffed with contraband. But when would she arrive? They had to know. Right now Gooch seemed the only chance. Any mistake in timing and they could miss it...

The stable door creaked open and two figures joined him in the darkness. Rackam's teeth gleamed as he broke into a smile.

"Two days from now, here at Upgang opposite the Mulgrave Castle Inn." He pointed to the shamble of well-lit buildings Hardiman had seen earlier. "There, on the beach. He says there're two caves behind the retaining wall. The goods'll be cached there before they're moved inland."

Relief flooded through Hardiman as he turned to see the Whitby officer examining his face. His brief smile had vanished to be replaced by his customary dourness.

"You were good in there," Rackam complimented, nodding. "You got the quickest results I've ever seen. For a moment there I almost believed you myself – Especially that bit about murdering him. That was a master touch." His face cracked into a genuine smile, then he lightly slapped Hardiman's back in congratulation.

Hardiman was grateful for the night. The darkness concealed his trembling hands.

*   *   *

The cottages of Whitby's west side thinned out quickly as Valentine and Jonathan Rudd walked the length of the outer harbour. At the end of the staith Valentine cast an eye over the twelve ancient eighteen-pound cannon lashed on the semi-circular battery, butting out over the beach. He wondered how many of them would blow to smithereens if they were ever fired. They turned to climb the cliff. At the top, the fields had burst into green with the coming of spring, promising a good harvest. Valentine turned to look at the harbour below, cluttered with lugsail cobbles, then the upper harbour where the whalers' masts stood in a thicket criss-crossed by briars of rigging.

"Their refits must be complete now," he ventured, indicating the whalers.

"Aye," Jonathan agreed. "They all sail about the same time, give or take a day or two. I've been ordered to ship aboard *Northern Star* on Friday, so that'll be our sailing day."

Valentine glanced at him. Just talking about it had given Jonathan a nervous smile. For a moment Valentine was envious. Off to the Greenland fishery where the whales swam among icebergs which stood out of the sea like great mountains of glass. What an adventure! No wonder Jonathan was excited.

Valentine smiled, dismissing his thoughts. He had no reason to be jealous. He had much more than Jonathan. Rapidly becoming important in Richard John's empire, he would soon be wealthy beyond his dreams. Things may be going badly for Richard John at the moment, but he had run his business along the same lines for nigh on twenty years. He was an old man. Valentine had never been so sure of that as the night they had crossed the River Tees, and old men don't move with the times. Valentine was sure the day would come when he would be invaluable to Richard John. Tom cared for nothing but hunting and made it plain he despised his father's trade. John himself said his son-in-law, Will Chapel, landlord of The Ship Inn, had not the brains to go further. That left only Margaret, and no smuggler would take orders from a woman. So, when the day came for Richard John to step down, Valentine was sure he'd be more than ready. He had already stored away ideas for improvement, and his mind was fertile. The sky was the limit. And then there was Margaret too. The thought of her made him ache...

"Aye, I dare say it'll be better than this spot."

Valentine banished his carnal daydreams. "I wish you luck."

Jonathan smiled proudly, seafaring blood awoken in his veins, then they continued the walk to Upgang. He pulled a weed stalk from the edge of the path and held up the yellow flower. "They say Greenlanders never see the summer here at Whitby all the years they sail."

Valentine shuddered. "Freezing in the Arctic and then suffering winter here, too."

Jonathan winked. "Aye, but if you catch fish aplenty, then your pockets are full of money and winter won't be so bad. I'll make even more brass, 'cause when I get back I'll still be going off with our Dad in *Speedwell*. Potting season'll be done, but there'll be plenty of cod."

They fell silent, plodding through the ankle high grass. A still day, the sun was so warm Valentine peeled off his coat and slung it over his shoulder. Ahead in the distance a large white house perched on the crumbling cliff.

"Castle Mulgrave Inn," Jonathan commented.

Closer, they halted then Jonathan pointed out routes across the land and where two storage caves were hidden by a seawall. Valentine stood for several minutes, trying to soak the terrain into his mind for the night two days hence when he would be here in pitch darkness. The more familiar now, the easier it would be then. Beside him, Jonathan wiped a wrist across his forehead.

Valentine glanced at the sky. "I'm thirsty. It's warm enough to melt tar." It wasn't thirst but nerves that parched his throat. His first run in command.

One slip and it could all go wrong.

*　　*　　*

It was bitterly cold. Wind shrieked through the rigging, snapping a slack halyard against the mainsail. Josiah Brown hated poor seamanship, but he suppressed his anger, waiting for the mate to notice the flogging rope. A cracked molar in his upper jaw aggravated his already foul mood. Rot had set in, producing a dull ache, occasionally exploding into a spike of screaming pain that drove up into his cheekbone until he wanted to tear off the whole side of his face. The beats of his pulse thudded through his head like the monotonous thump of a war-drum, bringing almost the same madness. He had worked at the tooth with his fingers, but it held fast as a kedging anchor on a rock shoal. When brandy had failed to numb the shattered molar, he almost sent for the carpenter's pliers... Only by sticking his tongue into what seemed an inch wide crevice in the tooth and constantly sucking, did he secure any relief. But the moment he stopped, pain flared again, destroying his temper, his concentration and his peace of mind.

"Are you going to tend to that or not?" Brown snapped, glaring at the mate who was talking with the helmsman.

He turned, frowning. "Aye aye, Cap'n." He stalked for'ard, glancing at the men checking the swivel guns. Not long now. They had already made landfall, a strand of lights climbing into the night on the port quarter which could only be Whitby. By dead reckoning, they were on a direct course to Upgang. "You there! Belay that halyard! Jump to it!" He watched a sailor attend the slack rope, then stood by the gunwale, hand resting on a marline spike. Glad to escape the captain's foul mood for a few moments, he twisted to stare at their wake. The moon was covered by scudding clouds and only the riding lights of a collier crawling across the horizon to northward could be seen. No danger there.

Morgan Butler rode low in the water, stacked to the hatches with gin and brandy, even the captain's tiny cabin commandeered to store bolts of silk and Flemish lace. Idly, the mate speculated on the ladies who would eventually wear gowns cut from them. Fine, well to do, likely as not, perfumed and elegant with gentle manners. And cold as ice. He hawked and spat over the side. No, not to his taste at all. He liked them warm and heavy breasted, a lusty twinkle in their eyes, with broad beamed buttocks so when you loosed your anchor they would tremble in your hands...

"Mr mate?! Are you conning this vessel or not?"

And damn you too, the mate thought as he retraced his steps to the quarterdeck. "You there! Stand by the lead. We'll start sounding soon." Beyond the helmsman, Josiah Brown was leaning on the starboard taffrail, staring into the night. He touched a hand to his face, slowly massaging his jaw. So, the mate thought, his tooth ache is back. That spelled a bad night. If only he had kept enough of his share in the profits, he could have bought his own lugger by now, but then the money never lasted. There was always another tavern and another wench... "Take a reef in there!" he called for'ard, eyes raking the billowing canvas. "Helmsman. Another two points to starboard." He glanced at Josiah Brown. "A clear run in, Cap'n."

Brown glanced at the men gathering sail and nodded, a glimmer of humour returning. "A clear run in's all I'm worried about. Once we're discharged, all the king's navy can board us if they care." He peered ahead at the dark shadow of land. "When you're ready, make the signal, and then heave to so's we can get it over with."

"Aye aye, Cap'n," the mate grinned, then *Morgan Butler* rose as a following wave lifted her transom, before dropping her into a trough. He began to call a stream of orders, stripping the sail from her. The tide pushed them shorewards while the men in the chains called soundings. Standing close in, the helm was put down and she headed up into the wind, steady while the signal lamp flashed. A watcher answered from the cliffs. The anchor splashed down in four fathoms, flukes bedding quickly. There was nothing to do then but wait for the boats to put out from the beach.

"I'm going below," Brown said, rubbing his jaw and stepping to the companion.

And I know what for, the mate thought. Toothache, hah. He could have done with a stiff tot himself. He hauled his coat close about him and buttoned it to cut the bitter wind rising off the wave tops. He opened his eyeglass and raked the shore. Yes, he could see them ploughing out. Two, no three. There should be more than that. They must be slow launching. Sea was bit tricky, mind. He compressed the glass and crossed the miniature quarterdeck. To seaward, whitecaps were building for the run in to the beach. He watched them idly for some minutes before he became aware of a pattern. A black shadow was moving across the sea, blotting out the rallying waves as it passed.

Then he understood. Oh, Jesus... He spun to the landward rail. The boats were near now. Still only three. Then he saw a spark. It could only be the reflection from a bayonet.

"Cut the anchor!" he shouted. "Loose the mains'l! Jump to it!" Faces turned toward him, confused. He grimaced. "It's a trap!"

TEN

"You can't do that," Rackam counselled.

"I can and I will, and what's more you'll help me." Hardiman was adamant. "With the extra Dragoons from York, the plan'll work."

Rackam interrupted. "We've got to catch them handling the cargo otherwise we've got no case. That's the law."

Hardiman laughed. "Law? D'you think those damned smugglers are playing by any rules?" He studied Rackam's dour face and sighed. "Look. You know who they are. I know who they are. The courts know who they are. Who's to say we didn't catch them red-handed? Doing it by the book we wait till they land some cargo, then move in. We both know that's the way we always lose them and most of the contraband too. There's a lot can go wrong tonight. We only need *Ferret* to turn up a few minutes late and we've lost the lugger. I saw it happen last time. Brown got clean away. This way we catch the smugglers on the beach while they're waiting to launch the boats. Then we'll row out and tackle the lugger. If *Ferret* turns up on time, then he gets his oar in too. If he's late we've saved the day."

The Whitby officer shook his head. "You're going to round up everyone on the beach? Just like that?"

"Come on! If they're on the beach at night, then they're up to no good. Admit it."

"I don't like it."

Hardiman persisted in trying to convince Rackam. "There'll be less bloodshed too. They won't believe we can arrest them without evidence. After we corner them your troopers can go through every man's house from top to bottom. You'll get your proof of complicity."

"I still don't like it."

"Rackam, you don't have to. You're playing against rogues. We have to play it their way whether we like it or not. This way we stand a chance of winning."

They split the Dragoons into three sections. Hardiman led one squad to sweep the beach from the lee of Whitby's west pier while his sergeant marshalled the second squad to sweep along Sandsend beach toward Whitby. Rackam, more familiar with the terrain, surrounded the Mulgrave Castle Inn and plugged the gaps along Upgang's low cliffs to prevent any smugglers escaping inland. After Rackam explained the Whitby men never used ponies when discharging cargo as most was stored in the vicinity then moved later, Hardiman decided both squads of Dragoons on the beach would close in on foot, silent, stripped of all unnecessary gear. It was imperative the lugger should not be warned of their presence. The plan was to keep their distance on the sands until the signal flashes were spotted, then spring the trap quickly.

Rackam nodded reluctantly. "We'll do it your way."

*   *   *

Richard John crouched in the long grass on the low cliff above Upgang Rocks. He could see the lights of the Mulgrave Castle Inn close by. He had been prepared to allow Valentine full authority over the run, but news had reached him Hardiman had left for Whitby. It didn't take much intelligence to deduce the Exciseman had sniffed something in the wind. And Hardiman was dangerous. Richard John decided to gather some men and watch from a discreet distance, then if help was needed, he was there. He believed in a little insurance. When he reached Hinderwell, word came a Customs Cutter was moored in

Runswick Bay, within easy striking distance of Whitby. The Upgang run was becoming more hazardous by the minute. But he was adamant he would not interfere. If Valentine could handle this situation, along with his other already discovered talents, then he would have proved his worth beyond doubt.

Or that was the theory. Reality was discomfort and nagging worry in the damp grass. His concentration, too, was wavering. Emotion had trespassed into his business plans. Hatred of Hardiman was overriding common sense. Being the king's man was despicable enough, but attempting to rape Margaret, his beloved daughter, was beyond forbearance. He had previously endured Hardiman's presence on the maxim of better the devil you know... but no longer. If the opportunity arose tonight, then Hardiman would pay, and he would pay heavily.

The men, gathered from Saltburn, Loftus and Runswick Bay were shadows in the night deployed around him. He had also taken the precaution of bringing six carts to move the contraband should it be necessary. But the waiting was excruciating. Then it struck him. This was the feeling he had missed for so long. Anticipation of excitement and danger coupled with the fear it all might go hideously wrong, and that lives would be lost. The realisation brought adrenaline rushing into his bloodstream. And he had thought himself bored with smuggling.

He smiled under cover of the night then froze as a man moved near him, a hand up for silence.

"Someone's coming," he whispered.

Harness on one of the cart horses jangled softly.

"Keep those horses quiet!" Richard John hissed.

*   *   *

"You know what to do. Cover any path which could provide an escape route from the beach." Officer Rackam looked both left and right at his Preventative Boatmen. "You each have a flare gun. Thompson has red and you, Howgego, have white. If the perpetrators outnumber you, fire a flare. The colour will show me where to send reinforcements. Any questions? No? Very well, carry on."

Thomas Howgego gestured to his six men and they separated from the main group to follow him westward along the cliff.

"Keep quiet," he muttered, fingering the unfamiliar flare gun in his belt. It was rubbing against his hip bone. He shifted it twice, then finally pulled it free to carry. There was a safety catch which his thumb grazed as he walked. On safe. He turned his attention to the meandering track. Once or twice he caught his toe, stumbling, cursing, but he soon fell into a rhythm, night vision becoming more acute. He wished fervently there would be no action on his section. Anyway, Hardiman and his Dragoons would catch them all on the beach. An hour or two and it would all be over and then they could all get home to bed.

"Stand fast or you're dead!"

Howgego was in mid stride. He faltered, missing his step, staggering.

"I said stand fast!"

A figure lurched at him from the ground. Howgego side-stepped and lost his footing. He saw the flash of a knife. Falling, he threw a hand in front of his face, his grip tightening convulsively.

With a whumph, a trail of smoke rocketed into the sky. Mouth agape, he stared at the gun in his hand then watched as high above him, the flare exploded into blinding white.

*   *   *

Valentine Rudd cursed. He stared into the barrel of Riding Officer Hardiman's pistol and cursed again. Everything had been under control. The men were organised, waiting on the beach to run down to the boats and push off into the breakers. Sheltering from the wind in the lee of the cliff, he had been whispering with Billy Rudd when signal flashes were spotted from *Morgan Butler*. Immediately, he ordered the reply, remembering it hadn't been so long ago when he lay in the grass on Saltburn's Cat Nab watching for the lugger. And now he was running the operation.

Then it fell to bits. Just as he was about to order the boats launched, the Dragoons appeared from the night. Within seconds Valentine's men were surrounded and disarmed. Hardiman moved in, wearing a wolf's head grin, then waved a cocked pistol under Valentine's nose.

"Well, I've got you now, and no mistake."

"For what?" Valentine replied, looking about him with open hands, brain desperately churning.

"I saw the signal and I saw your answer. Your illegal cargo is sitting out there on the *Morgan Butler*. Only Captain Brown is about to get a little surprise." He glanced at the Dragoon sergeant who had just completed his beach sweep from Sandsend. "Mount guard here. They're under arrest." He jerked his head at Valentine. "Keep a special eye on this one. He belongs to me. If anyone is going to put a musketball through him while he's attempting to escape, then it'll be me."

Valentine watched the Riding Officer lead a squad of Dragoons down the beach to the cobles at the tide line, the last thrust of the breakers dying beneath grounded keels. He realised then what Hardiman had in mind. Somehow he had to warn Captain Brown. He felt helpless. Without a weapon, how? He thought frantically, but could find no solution, and time was passing. They had already launched through the surf and were pulling hard for the anchored lugger.

Then the flare went off. It climbed into the sky over Upgang

Beach and burst magnesium bright, spilling a pool of white light almost a hundred yards wide over the sands.

*   *   *

Hardiman huddled in the sternsheets of a coble, hat hidden beneath his cloak, counting oar strokes as they closed with *Morgan Butler*. When the flare soared into the night sky and burst, he twisted to stare back at the beach. Rackam was in trouble. Hardiman glanced sharply at the lugger when he heard the thud of an axe, then the severed anchor hawser roared out and disappeared into the sea. Canvas was being hauled up, slatting against the masts.

"Pull!" he called, decision made. Rackam had the Dragoons on the beach to help him, but if the lugger escaped there was no evidence. Bare yards now, but *Morgan Butler* was already gathering way. The crew busy setting sail, the swivel guns were unmanned. Feet now. She rose above them, masts taller by the second, then the boat nudged her. The deck stood an arm's length above the coble. Hardiman drew his hangar and gripped it between his teeth like a pirate, then clambered up and over. Half a dozen men were at his back. He drew his pistol, cocked the hammer then pulled the trigger.

Men at the rigging dropped halyards to draw cutlasses. In moments the deck was a mass of fighting men, blades rasping and pistols exploding under a welter of hoarse cries.

Josiah Brown abandoned his brandy glass when he heard the mate's shout. Grabbing his weapons he climbed the companion. "Stand to the helm!" he shouted.

"Look yonder!" the mate pointed to starboard.

Brown grimaced. "King's cutter. Man that gun." He gestured at the port swivel while he leaned over the starboard weapon, gripping the trigger lanyard. "*Butler's!* Fall back to the mainmast!" The mob amidships parted, the crew obeying him instantly.

Brown swung the gun to port where the king's men stood on a section of captured deck. He yanked the lanyard and the swivel spat a long tongue of flame and sparks. A hundred musket balls tore through the Dragoons. Brown held up his hand to prevent the mate firing, then smoke drifted to reveal a group of broken, bloodied men. "You want more? No, then over the side with you!"

Miraculously, Hardiman was untouched. He examined his shattered men. Half had fallen to the grapeshot. The remainder were stunned, staring unbelieving at their fallen comrades. Two more charges from the swivels and they would all be dead. Brown had only lost one or two. "Back to the boats," he muttered, throat dry.

Awash with wounded, the boat pushed shoreward. Behind, the lugger heeled under drawing sails. "I'll get you, Brown! Mark my words!" Hardiman shouted defiantly.

*   *   *

Valentine stared at the exploding flare, then switched his attention to the circle of Dragoons round his men. They were distracted. He tapped Billy's shoulder, then lunged at the nearest trooper. He wrenched a musket aside then jerked his knee into the soldier's groin. When he folded, Valentine used the weapon as a club to lay him out. All around him, the smugglers were fighting for their freedom, breaking heads and shedding blood. He glimpsed the sergeant struggling with Billy. Stepping in, he grabbed hold and flung him to the ground. When Billy moved to knock him out, Valentine stopped him. Instead, he twisted the sergeant's neck stock, choking him.

"The flare. What does it mean?"

The Irishman stared back, lips tight.

"Use that musket to blow one of his knees off," Valentine ordered Billy.

The sergeant's eyes narrowed as the steel muzzle prodded his kneecap, gauging the value of his leg against the information. "It means there's trouble on the cliff."

"How many up there?" When the Irishman faltered Valentine snarled: "I mean business. I'll do for both your legs."

"Officer Rackam and ten troopers." When Valentine shook his neck like a dog the sergeant blurted. "That's all, sor. 'Tis the truth."

Valentine dropped him and stood up. "Tie him." Since the flare had burned out, the beach seemed darker. From what he could see, his men were winning. Offshore, flashes of gunfire gave away *Morgan Butler's* position. No cargo now. "Any of our men on the cliff, Billy? No? Well, who's fighting the Exciseman up there?"

Within minutes, the captors had become the captured, herded into a circle. Valentine picked out three of the Whitby men. "Tie them up then follow us. The rest, come with me. Billy, you lead, you know the way." He started for the cliff.

*   *   *

"What's going on there?" Lt-Commander James Major muttered, staring across black water at the smuggling lugger which had begun to swing, shadows climbing her masts as sails were hauled up.

The mate cursed. "She's cut her cable to run." A crackle of gunfire and shouting carried across the water. The mate grimaced. "I reckon she's being boarded. I'd lay money on it."

"Hardiman," Major said grimly. He glanced the length of the deck, *Ferret* running silently on shortened sail down toward *Morgan Butler*. It would have been perfect but for the Exciseman. "Make sail," he ordered, reaching for the speaking trumpet. "Ahoy there! Heave-to in the King's name!"

The mate stared. The captain was still doing it by the book.

"Starboard guns! Fire as you bear!" Major shouted, melting the mate's astonishment into a grin. The four-pounders began to bellow one after another, balls howling across the oily sea.

"Mark the fall of shot!" the mate called, powder smoke blinding the quarterdeck. *Ferret* was closing steadily. Tongues of flame belched from the lugger then grape shot peppered the cutter's sails. "He's shooting high," the mate gloated. "I believe we have the better of him." *Ferret's* cannon spewed thunder again. Holes appeared in the lugger's sails and white wood splintered from the bulwarks before the smuggler's swivel guns replied again. There were screams for'ard as a hail of lead ripped through a gun crew.

They were close now, *Ferret* driven by bloated sails, froth bubbling from her forefoot. The mate calculated the distance. Approaching at an angle to present the thinnest silhouette, *Ferret* should now be swinging to port. He looked at Major who seemed to be engrossed. "Helm, sir," he prompted.

"Hold her steady!" Major barked, eyes welded to the lugger.

The mate estimated the distance again. They should sheer away now. "Sir, there's not much time."

"I said hold her steady! That's an order!"

It was then the mate knew what Major had intended all along.

*   *   *

Hardiman hunched in the sternsheets, anger making him oblivious to the coble's jerky progress. Without enough oarsmen fit to crew the boat, it lurched through the breakers. The wounded moaned continuously, huddled in misery down on the duckboards. What now, he wondered, then flinched as cannonfire erupted. Expecting grapeshot to scythe over his head, Hardiman half turned to squint back. The lugger's near side was quiet, then he saw the hole in her for'ard sail. As he watched, debris was blown clear off the deck, scattering into the sea. But *Morgan Butler's* canvas was filling as she slowly gathered way to run Eastward. As she drew clear, a vessel emerged on her far side, cannon blazing, running down fast, sails brimming with wind.

"*Ferret*," he mumbled. So Major had arrived in time after all. It was impossible for the smuggler to outrace the flying cutter. One problem solved; another to face. Rackam's flare. He glanced at the Dragoons slumped at the oars, wondering how many would be fit to fight when they landed. Suddenly the coble slewed, a wave smashing her stern quarter, spray showering the boat. Almost beam ends on to the following wave, she barely escaped broaching. The oarsmen's blades were trailing in the rebellious sea, useless. "Port oars rest! Starboard oars! Pull!" he shouted. The coble righted, her bows again to the land. "All stroke! Now!"

In minutes she grounded and they left her wallowing at the breaker line. A ragged mob, trailing weapons, they started up the beach. Under the cliff they found the prisoners' guard trussed like baggage, mouths stuffed with rags. As they were freed, Hardiman listened to the sounds of fighting above and glanced back at cannonfire flashing over the sea. The lugger was obviously still in range of *Ferret's* broadside.

"On your feet, man," he grumbled at the sergeant. "What happened?"

"They overcame us when that flare went off. They went up the cliff, sor. But who's fighting up there? I don't understand."

Hardiman frowned. "Get your men. You're about to find out."

*   *   *

Night hung in a thick blanket over the clifftop. Valentine faintly saw the outline of the Mulgrave Castle Inn as he stumbled the last few feet. Off to his right a musket barked, aimed inland. He marked the flash, then sword in hand covered the coarse grass until he discerned the dim form of a man. He was facing away, laying on his side, reloading. Valentine crept towards him, then abruptly dropped a knee into his back, cutlass poised above a vulnerable throat.

"Who are you and who're you fighting?"

Billy had followed. "I know him. Gooch, what's going on?"

The informer Jack Gooch relaxed as the cutlass was removed. "I was up here as look-out when Rackam and the Dragoons arrived. They surrounded the inn, then they were attacked. Men from Saltburn I think."

"Where are they?"

"Over there." A scrawny arm indicated the right flank.

Valentine gestured. "Show us the way." Gooch rose, then crabbed through the undergrowth, Valentine and Billy at his heels. A pistol cracked, a ball whistling over Valentine's head. A volley of muskets answered from both left and right. "Where?" Valentine shouted, close to Gooch's ear. The informer waved toward the inn. Valentine patted his shoulder then set off at a half run, dodging bushes.

"Stand still, or I'll shoot you down!" Valentine froze. "Oh, it's you. Get down," a burly Saltburn fisherman growled.

Richard John was hunched in deep shadow by the wheel of a cart. "Wondered when you'd get here. A bit o'noise and I knew you'd come running. What kept you?" He was smiling.

Valentine strained his eyes, searching the shadows. "Some Dragoons on the beach got in my way. But what are you doing here?" Another volley of shots drove Valentine to his knees so he could hear the reply.

"Something smelled funny, so I came to lend a hand. As neat a trap as I've ever seen."

"My first run without you and it goes wrong." Valentine commented bitterly.

Richard John placed a hand on his shoulder. "Everyone

learns the hard way. There's no use to it now. Cap'n Brown'll cut his anchor and run. We'd best do the same... Look out!"

A line of Dragoons on horseback swept out of the night, trampling all in their way. Valentine remembered the cavalry's precision manoeuvres on Saltburn beach and knew it was impossible to beat them.

"Get those carts out of here!" John bellowed, green eyes flashing as he stood to meet the charge, a pistol in each hand. "Fall back then split up and run! Get to it!" He discharged a pistol at the nearest rider. The Dragoon yelled, pulling the charger up short. The pistol ball had torn a ragged hole in his chest, a powder burn smeared across white crossbelts. As he tumbled from the saddle, already dead, his shifting weight slewed the horse round. Half rearing, rear hooves shuffled for a hold on the grass while both forefeet churned the air.

Richard John was too close and too slow. A steel horseshoe smashed into his shoulder. Flung backward, he collided with the cart, legs collapsing. At that moment the carter goaded his pony forward. A Dragoon galloped past, sabre swinging. The blade sliced open a fountain of blood from the carter's chest. The second slash, misaimed, felled the pony. Hooves scrabbling, the cart was pushed backward as the animal fell whinnying in the traces. Richard John sprawled on the ground in a daze, then screamed as an iron-bound wheel rolled slowly backward onto his chest. Desperately, he grabbed at the spokes, his strength crushed, no contest for the heavy vehicle and the dead pony.

Valentine was fighting for his life. Instead of running, the smugglers had closed ranks about him and were standing off the Dragoons' assault. He swung the cutlass again and again, parrying blows almost wrenching his arm from its socket. Strength draining fast, time meant nothing as the night yielded skirmish after skirmish. Hair plastered to his forehead, shirt soaked, Valentine fought on. He had two options. Die or be taken prisoner. He decided to fight to the end.

One moment he was fighting. The next the Dragoons had vanished back into the night. The lull provided breathing space to take stock of the bodies tangled in the clumps of grass. Surprised, he realised he had edged almost fifty yards from the cart. Retracing his steps, he wondered why it was still there. Closer, he saw the dead pony and the carter sprawled across the seat. He leaned against it, gulping to replenish starving muscles. He frowned when he heard a groan, then stooped to peer under the wagon bed.

"Mr John?" He groped, hands closing on the wheel rim embedded in the smuggler's chest. "I'll free you." He began to hack at the pony's traces with his cutlass. Once the dead animal was released he should be able to roll the cart forward. The leathers parted and he lifted the shafts vertical to prevent them digging into the earth. At the side, he put his shoulder to the wheel. He grunted with effort, but it refused to move. He strained until veins threatened to burst from his forehead. Breathless, he stood drooping.

"Son?" The smuggler's mouth twisted with pain. "You'll never move it. The axle's broken." Valentine grimaced then knelt to feel under the wagon. It was true. He needed horses and men. As he stood up a rocket hissed into the sky, arcing directly overhead before exploding into blinding white.

"Christ," Valentine muttered, shielding his eyes as the clifftop was illuminated bright as day. On the far side of the light's circle a skirmish line of horses and Dragoons was visible. As the flare continued to burn, Valentine saw two men in black at the centre of the line. One began to shout. "Prepare to advance!"

"It's Hardiman," Richard John mumbled. "They've got us now. Run."

Valentine shook his head. "No." He put his shoulder to the wheel again in a last futile effort.

"Stop, lad."

"And leave you? No." A vice-like hand grabbed his ankle.

"Run, I said. Run and fight another day. My time has been and gone. It's down to men like you now." The smuggler grimaced. "Remember what I said? Sunset be glory." When Valentine still shook his head, John prodded. "There's Margaret to think about. Who'll look after her?"

"Troopers! Forward!" Hardiman's voice bellowed.

The hand shook Valentine's ankle urgently. "Go, and be quick about it. I'll think none the less of you." He grinned weakly. "Besides, I don't allow anyone to save my life twice."

Valentine still hestitated. Hope sparked as the flare died, plunging the clifftop back into darkness. Within a second, another roared into the sky to banish the night. Valentine knelt and clasped Richard John's hand. There seemed so much to say, yet he said nothing. Their eyes locked until the smuggler's closed. His grip tightened as pain wrenched his innards, then he let go.

"Run," he whispered, exhausted.

When Valentine vanished into the night, Richard John groped until he found one of his pistols. Shakily, he held it close to his face, smiling as he saw it was still charged. Thank God. If Hardiman came within range, then he would shoot the black hearted bastard down. Perhaps it would staunch the anguish for what Margaret had suffered. He heard the hooves then, rumbling through the earth. If only he could resist the pain a little longer. Even five minutes. Involuntarily his eyes squeezed closed again. He had such plans. Under his guidance, and with the boy's brains, there were no limits to what they could accomplish. But he had to stay alive. And Hardiman had to die.

It happened like a nightmare. The Dragoons galloped out of the night, Riding Officers at their head. For a second he feared they would ride right over him, then the line split to veer down either side of the stranded cart. The stallion ran right into Richard John's gunsight. The smuggler levelled the pistol and pulled the trigger. The flash and powder smoke blinded him for an instant. But the stallion galloped onward, Hardiman shouting and waving his sword.

The ball had missed.

*   *   *

Josiah Brown gave a spare grin as the repelled boarders fled over the side. The instant they were gone, he forgot them. "Make sail!" he shouted, flinching as the cold wind probed his shattered molar. *Morgan Butler* was making way, but not enough. The men who had fought returned to the halyards, falling into a line to haul up canvas.

"Ahoy there! Heave-to in the King's name!"

Brown faced the cutter looming from the night. His tongue sucked at his aching tooth while he estimated speeds and distance. He glanced at the slapping sails and knew he had no leeway. The cutter was running down too fast. *Morgan Butler* would either have to withstand a broadside as the cutter passed, or the king's man was going to haul his wind and try to board. Brown could not steer inshore without grounding. He would have to brazen it out and run straight past the cutter.

Thunder boomed, flashes rippling along the cutter's flank. A ball howled overhead, smacking through the mainsail. Brown grunted, then cursed as another ball ploughed into a bulwark amidships, scattering the men working the canvas. Smoking, it careered across the deck and smashed through the topsides, spewing debris into the sea. "Fire the swivels!" He jerked the lanyard nearest to him. Nothing happened. It had not been reloaded since he fired at the boarders. Further for'ard, other swivel guns crashed. They had little effect. The cutter still bore down. Brown was puzzled. The king's man should be spilling his wind now if he intended to board. And physics dictated if he maintained the same course they would collide. Even if adjustments were made at the last minute and the cutter sheered away, opposing forces in the sea would drag them together.

Another broadside thundered from the cutter's four-pounders. It seemed cannonballs were raining onto the smuggler's frail timbers. One smashed through the quarterdeck bulwark, throwing up a screen of wood splinters. Brown ducked as the ball screamed past him, the splinters whirling through the air. One caught his coat, tearing his right pocket away. *Morgan Butler* began to crab, the wind swinging abeam to drive her ashore.

"Hold her steady!" he bawled then twisted to see the helmsman spinning the loose wheel.

"Rudder ropes've gone, Cap'n."

Brown cursed. Where was escape now? And holds stuffed to the hatches with contraband. He tried to fathom out some sort of solution but amid the explosions of gunfire and the throbbing from his aching tooth, his thoughts seemed clogged and muddy. He cast uselessly about. *Morgan Butler* was drifting now. He glanced again at the cutter. Her sails were still bloated with wind, her course steady. The Customs man could not know the lugger was crippled, and suddenly it was clear he had intended ramming from the start. Well, if Brown couldn't cut and run, then he would fight his vessel as hard as he knew how.

Stubbornly, he began to reload the swivel. If he could only rid himself of toothache, then he could think his way out. Mechanically, he cleaned the bore then packed cartridge, wad and charge. As he forced it home the lugger lurched. *Ferret's* bowsprit punched into her port bow. Timbers everywhere shrieked a protest. Taut rigging snapped and flailed the deck like whips. The cutter's momentum hauled *Morgan Butler* up out of the water, men rolling down her tilted deck in a tumble of loose gear into the scuppers. After the initial noise collapsed into silence, the groan of the mainmast was audible as it swayed then cracked and toppled slowly over the side, canvas, rigging and all.

Josiah Brown's feet had gone from under when they were rammed. His chin caught the swivelgun as he fell, triggering a pain like lightning which screamed from his shattered tooth up through his cheekbone, almost blinding him with agony. Howling with rage, he hauled himself to his feet as he heard the call: "Boarders away!"

Then they were streaming over his gunwales. The king's men, armed to the teeth with cutlasses and pistols, boarding axes and pikes. Eyes slitted, Brown watched them come. He took hold of the lanyard and aimed the swivel carefully, measuring the field of his fire to maximise the spreading effect of the deadly charge. Certain, he jerked the trigger.

The swivel gun exploded, the barrel bursting like a flower. He was flung backwards. The taffrail slammed into his back and he landed awkwardly, arms and legs at impossible angles. He had no idea what had happened, only there was something wrong with his limbs. They would not obey. He grimaced, exerting his will. The strain sent pain skewering through his stomach. He looked down. His coat and shirt were shredded, embedded in a red glutinous mess. Horror dawned as he realised it was his stomach. His breeches were sodden, a ruptured artery spilling dark blood on the deck around him.

He knew it was the end. He had seen enough men die to know. If so, he was determined he would take as many of them with him as he could. Josiah Brown concentrated then, inching a hand to a pistol laid nearby. He frowned when a strange roaring began in his head, like the ocean roused to storm pitch. He listened for a moment, smiling, then slowly his head lolled back against the rail, open eyes staring unseeing at the night sky.

For'ard, the mate struggled to free himself from a coil of cordage. "Repel boarders!" he shouted, rising to his feet. Where was the captain? He should be commanding the counter attack. The mate rallied the confused crew and as they started fighting hand to hand, he edged back to the quarterdeck. He found Josiah Brown sitting dead in a pool of his own blood. The mate's shoulders slumped, his cutlass trailing on the deck.

"Mother of God," a voice muttered at his shoulder and he turned to see one of the crew making the sign of the cross. Before he could stop him, the sailor turned and shouted. "The cap'n's dead! Cap'n Brown's dead!"

For'ard, the smugglers fell back, staring at the quarterdeck. They would not fight without their captain to lead them. One man threw down his cutlass onto the deck. Another followed. Within a minute they had all surrendered. The mate watched them. It was all over.

*   *   *

The night was full of demons. Valentine ran, men straggling either side seeking refuge under the shield of darkness. He was confused, unable to hear the breakers on the beach because of his breath sawing in his lungs. He could only pray he was running inland toward safety. Behind him, horses crashed through the scrub. A pistol barked then a mount neighed, mixed with the rasp of swordplay. Valentine paused, half crouching, chest heaving. Peering back he could see nothing. The Dragoons must be rounding up the smugglers. They were close. He flinched as another figure loomed from the darkness to stagger past him, unrecognisable. Nothing to do but run as far and as fast as possible. When things quietened he could circle back and make for Whitby. Still gasping, he noted where the moon stood in the sky and gathered his bearings. No alternative. He pushed himself back into a muscle-numbing run, knees buckling. It seemed he had a chance...

Then the horseman came out of the night. The black stallion overtook him, hooves thudding hollowly. Valentine twisted his head up to see the glossy flanks of the horse. Oh God, Hardiman. Valentine shambled to a halt, groping for his pistol, but found his waistband empty. The riding officer hauled the black to a standstill, moonlight gleaming from the hangar dangling from his hand. The horse backed, tossing his head, snorting steamy breath, eyes rolling. Valentine watched the foam dripping from the stallion's mouth as it gnashed at the bit, then switched to Hardiman.

The Exciseman wore a wolf's head grin, madness in his eyes. He spurred the black forward, guiding it with his knees so the animal weaved from side to side, Valentine retreating under its advance.

"Now, boy, it's your turn."

Valentine lacked the energy to reply. His legs seemed rooted and he wearily prised them from the earth to evade the horse. He drew his cutlass, blade still smeared with blood from earlier encounters. Muscles drained, the weapon hung from his hand. The stallion's shoulders bunched, head down, kept in check as Hardiman prolonged the advance.

Then Valentine knew. In control, Hardiman felt secure. Always use your head, Richard John had said time and again. If the opposition has the initiative, take it away from them. As Valentine continued to back off, he focused all his concentration on horse and rider.

Without warning, Valentine lunged, sword arm slashing. The blade ripped across the stallion's neck drawing a gout of blood. The black flinched and twisted away, neighing. Hardiman fought to control him, his own mouth gurning with anger. He kicked free of the stirrups. As the stallion veered sideways, he leapt from the saddle. Valentine staggered then went down when the Exciseman crashed into him. Both men lost their weapons, Hardiman's spinning away into the grass, Valentine's torn from his hand to fall near his head. Strength born of desperation surged into exhausted muscles. He pushed the Exciseman off, then scrambled for the cutlass.

Hardiman was there too. Grunting and cursing, they punched wildly at each other while trying to grab the blade. Rolling across the grass, Valentine fought his way on top, hands gripping the Exciseman's throat.

"Now you'll pay," Valentine muttered from between clenched teeth. "I won't leave you alive this time." A fist crashed into his ribs, tipping him sideways. Then they were brawling again, hands tearing at each other as they battled for the upper hand.

Valentine was tiring fast. Each skirmish left him weaker, breathless, muscles screaming. Hardiman seemed to sense his failing strength, renewing the attack even more vigorously. Slowly, Valentine felt his defence collapse until he barely stopped the Exciseman from throttling him. Finally, Hardiman had a hold on his windpipe that erased everything but the need to breathe. As he rolled onto his back, Hardiman came astride him, pinning him to the grass. Valentine could see no escape. His strength had fled.

The Exciseman was grinning, face thrust to within inches of his victim. Valentine lay still, hoping to lull him into relaxing his stranglehold.

"This is it, the end, "Hardiman sneered. "There's no more. You die here. Richard John is finished too. And I'll go back to Saltburn and have his daughter. I'll finish what you interrupted..." His head jerked back, astonishment written on his face. "Oh no, how did you... How?" His eyes seemed frozen in a distant stare before glazing over. All expression melted from his features as his grip failed, fingers twitching in spasms as they left Valentine's throat. Slowly, he keeled over to sprawl face down on the grass.

It was only then Valentine saw the man standing above them. Struggling up onto his elbows, he saw the hangar sticking up from Hardiman's back.

The man leaned down, offering a hand to pull him up. Upright, he realised the newcomer was a small man, wiry, with lank hair. He peered at the man's face. "You're Jack Gooch. You were at the top of the cliff."

The informer was staring down at the Exciseman.

"You've killed him," Valentine added lamely.

"I owed him," Gooch said without regret, hawking a gob of

phlegm to spit on the ground. Then he looked over his shoulder. "Follow me. The rest of the Dragoons'll be here soon."

Valentine took one last look at the Riding Officer, then together, they disappeared into the night.

*   *   *

The sergeant found the stallion first. Wandering in circles, gore had dripped from its neck down both forelegs, matting a once glossy coat. It was head down, on trembling legs. The sergeant called for Rackam then they continued the search. After some minutes they found a trail of flattened grass smeared with blood. They followed it on foot to where Hardiman lay twisted on his side, the hanger still protruding from his back.

The Irish sergeant tore off his own neck stock and rolled it into a ball, then looked at Rackam. "When I pull out the blade, plug the hole straight away."

Rackam nodded and took the cloth. He grimaced as the sergeant took a grip on the hilt, twisting it slightly to release the suction before drawing it slowly free. Hardiman groaned, eyes opening briefly before he sank into unconsciousness.

Rackam looked at the sergeant who shook his head. He had seen too many wounds to be optimistic. They carried Hardiman back to Whitby and the sergeant sat through the night with him. When Rackam entered the room at dawn the sergeant had already pulled the blanket over Hardiman's head.

"Did he say anything?"

The sergeant was grim. "Only two words. Valentine Rudd." Rackam nodded. "I understand."

*   *   *

"But I've got to go to Saltburn," Valentine stated, shading his eyes from the morning sun as he looked downstream. Below the draw-bridge a crowd was gathered at the staithe. Beside him, Billy Rudd shook his head brusquely.

"No. We'll talk later, when our Jonathan's got off." He patted his son's shoulder. Jonathan smiled back, a hand resting on his sea chest while they waited for the bridge to lower so they could cross the harbour. "Sailing Day is special, moreso for a lad going off for the first time." Billy glanced at his wife who was wearing a stiff face, bracing herself to say good-bye when her son left for the Greenland Fishery.

"Give me one good reason," Valentine argued.

Billy sighed. "I've told you. I had news last night from Saltburn. Richard John's behind bars at York Castle. A doctor strapped him up and they wouldn't allow his family to see him. His house is swarming with soldiers and Excisemen. They were chuffed they got the *Morgan Butler* and her cargo, but they were madder than hell that we got away. Especially you. Rackam is spitting blood and searching for you. He holds you responsible for Hardiman's death."

Valentine had heard that, but did not believe it. Why should they think he was to blame? Nobody could have seen what happened. And if they had, they would know Jack Gooch was the murderer. "I must see Margaret," he said, determined.

Billy made a face, producing an envelope from his pocket. "She knows you're safe. She sent this."

Valentine glanced at her handwriting, then stuffed it inside his coat. "I'll read it later," he said, eyes watching the ropes lowering the bridge. "Here." He grabbed one end of Jonathan's chest to help him carry it across the harbour, then along the quay to where *Northern Star* was berthed. Close to the whaler they had to push through the milling crowd of relatives where the Greenlanders were enduring final hugs and tearstained kisses. One by one, they turned to go aboard, shouting their names as they set foot on the gangplank to be recorded by the bos'un. Valentine glanced up at the crew lining the gunwales and recognised several faces from the run at Upgang. One or two met his eyes and nodded, then looked away.

Northern Star was a solid vessel, 95 feet overall and 200 tons. Three masts raked the sky, garlands and pennants fluttering from the topgallant mast truck above the crow's nest. Her wide yards, each bearing a coil of furled canvas, overhung the staithe, both running and standing rigging humming a low melody of eagerness in the freshening breeze. Thoroughly overhauled through the winter, her scraped and tallowed hull would make her as fleet as she would ever be when she fled the harbour for the run north to the whaling grounds. There was a tautness, a readiness about her, that stirred something in Valentine. He turned to look at Jonathan who suddenly seemed even younger somehow. His mother was ticking off points on her fingers, Jonathan listening with edgy patience. She brought out a pair of mitts secretly made. Her son smiled then stuffed them in a pocket and kissed her cheek. She held him tight a moment, then Billy Rudd grinned and shook his son's hand before Valentine wished him luck and a safe journey home.

"Jonathan Rudd, apprentice!" he shouted, mounting the gang plank, struggling with his sea chest.

"Come aboard, Mr Rudd!"

Jonathan joined the line of men at the gunwale laughing and waving to their relatives. He looked raw and innocent next to the sea-worn faces and easy smiles. With a grate, the gangplank was being hauled in and the first mate was shouting from the quarterdeck.

"All hands aboard! Prepare to warp out! Cast off for'ard! Ready with the nippers!" It rose to a bellow. "Look lively! Bos'un, pay attention to the starboard watch there! I'll not be made a fool of in my home port! Away aloft! Shake out those courses!"

A hawser from *Northern Star's* bridal port lay carefully along the staithside flagging. A line of men stood over it, hands on hips, watching the Greenlanders race up the ratlines then edge out on the footropes along the yards to free the furling lines. Loosed, the sails sagged, still creased, empty of wind. Almost as one, the men ashore bent and took hold of the warp, gathering tension ready for the order. Somewhere amid the confusion of commands was one they obeyed. In step, they tramped towards the vessel's stern, the hawser groaning taut round a bollard to lever *Northern Star* out into the river current where she could gain steerage way. Her sails rippled, gnawing at the breeze as she shied away from the staithe. There was logic in the seeming chaos which impressed Valentine, crushed in the waving crowd.

"Make way! Make way there!"

Frowning, Valentine spun round. Complaining families were being pushed aside. As a gap opened he caught sight of the agitators. An Exciseman flanked by Dragoons carrying muskets. The Officer's face swung into view. Rackam. Valentine scanned the perimeter of the crowd. Above their heads he saw sun glinting on a stockade of bayonets. He was completely surrounded. The onlookers were parting quickly, bullied and threatened. Valentine cast about, searching for escape. There was none. Next to him, Billy was shielding his wife as he strained to see over the crowd.

"What now?"

Billy's eyes met his. "The water. It's the only way."

Fear sparked in Valentine's eyes. "No."

"You've no choice."

Valentine twisted to look at *Northern Star* lumbering into the harbour. She was already seven or eight feet from the staithe. Too far to jump. He looked back over his shoulder. Rackam had seen him and was half running, shouting, waving a white parchment.

"Valentine Rudd! I have a warrant here for your arrest! Give yourself up!" Then the parchment was stuffed inside his coat and a pistol appeared in his hand.

"Jump lad!" Billy urged.

Indecision rooted Valentine to the spot. Why a warrant for him and not for Billy? It had to be Hardiman's death. So it was true, they really were blaming him. One glance at Rackam's face convinced him the authorities had already made up their mind. Guilty. And murder meant hanging. But he was innocent! Yet he was wise enough to realise there were no alibis this time, false or otherwise... His eyes flickered back to *Northern Star* as a gap opened on the lip of the staithe. He glimpsed Jonathan's face at the whaler's gunwale, his arms open wide, beckoning.

"Stop or I shoot!" Rackam bawled.

Valentine sprinted. Ten strides. Then he launched himself into space. *Northern Star's* solid timbers smashed the breath from his chest. Hands grabbed at him but his coat tore away. Body out of control, his fingers clawed splinters as he slid down the planking. His knees jerked and scraped raw, body twisting as he fell. Ears deaf to the shouting on the quay behind him, he was ignorant of the musket ball thudding into the ship's oak inches from his head. Then he plunged into the harbour.

The water was bitterly cold. Numbing arms wrapped themselves tightly round Valentine's shoulders to pull him down into the darkness. As he sank, an iron band round his ribs squeezed the air from his lungs. Hair flowing round his head, open eyes blinded by the mixture of fresh and salt water, Valentine felt the bubbles of life escaping his mouth. They burst past his head to race for the surface. He began to flap his arms and kick out with all the strength he could summon, but he continued to sink. He seemed to be spinning head over heels, panic hammering in his eardrums, fear a sharp pain in his chest. Not that he thought about it then, for there was no time to think clearly. Drowning had always been accepted as an occupational hazard. Most men who fought the sea's unpredictable moods eventually gave their lives back to it in the end, fair trade perhaps for all the food they had taken from her. In an accident far out off the coast, swimming would only prolong the inevitable. Few ever learned, and Valentine was not one of the few...

God, it was cold. It struck through his skin and bones like spears of ice, cold as death. Harbour weed caressed his face, seeking to embrace him. Oh God, he was going to die...

Then he was tearing at his riding boots. One came off, sinking as soon as it was loose. His free leg felt light as a feather as his hands wrenched and tugged frantically at the other. The pain in his chest was unbearable now, a screaming knife slicing wickedly, twisting, impaling him. Water invaded his mouth as he struggled. Gagging, he forced his fingers into the gap between the leather and his calf then eased the boot down as quickly as he could without snagging it. The pain was like a fork of lightning now, burning down through his chest, white-hot fire that seared away even the water's cold grip. And his nose was in the jaws of a vice, rough woollen fingers stuffed up his nostrils, pressuring to claw inside his head. He was twisting and spinning in the dark water, death only a breath away. He felt a slackening near his ankle, wet leather sliding free, and he began to hope. But the harbour was reluctant to give him up, tendrils of brine worming past his lips, trickling down his throat into the furnace of his lungs. Pain, oh pain...

The boot came off, then he was kicking, arms scrabbling, a silent scream in his head as he rose. Would he never reach the surface? Upwards, slowly, like in a dream. He could see *Northern Star's* giant shadow, gliding out of reach. A nightmare of terror and bursting lungs and fists gouging from behind his eyes, forcing them from their sockets. A howl in his brain. *Stay away, Reaper, I want to live.*

He burst through the surface head flung back, mouth agape, coughing and spluttering. Air! Sweet air, driving into his bruised and punished lungs. Gagging, spewing seawater. But air, the delicious pain of it. His eyes cleared to the brilliance of sunshine reflected from the harbour water. It had been so murky down there but up here it was beautiful. He blinked as water ran down from his hair.

"Valentine! Here!"

Jonathan was at *Northern Star's* gunwale, a painter hanging in a coil from his hand. He swung it back then flung it out over the water, splashing down within reach. Valentine foundered then caught it gratefully. Relaxing momentarily, he went back under. He threw his head back when the tide scoured his nostrils. Then hands were pulling at the rope, dragging him toward the whaler. His raw palms flattened against her timbers then they hauled him up the topsides by the main chains and over the gunwale onto the deck. He collapsed in a heap, dripping, exhausted, resting a minute on hands and knees before he staggered upright.

Back on the staithe the crowd had pulled back, leaving Rackam alone in a clearing, waving his pistol. "I've a warrant! I claim him!"

"If you discharge that weapon at my ship again, I shall be obliged to return your fire!" a voice threatened from the quarterdeck. Valentine turned to see an officer, hands clasped behind his back, head set between his shoulders like a bulldog as he glowered at the Exciseman.

"Good old Cap'n Falton," the bos'un grinned.

With every second, the whaler edged further from the quay. Her sails were luffing as they sought to gather wind.

"Cast off the warp!" Falton called, then glanced amidships. "Bring that man here!"

Along with the bos'un and Jonathan, Valentine slopped to the quarterdeck. The captain looked him up and down. "A bit wet behind the ears no doubt," he said dryly, "but have you shipped aboard before?"

Valentine was confused. "I'm a fisherman by trade, but I don't want to sail..."

"I think you're a Greenlander now, lad," Falton interrupted

bluntly. "I'm a man or two short. Mind, if you don't want to go I can always land you back ashore. I'm sure that gentleman would welcome you back." He followed Valentine's glance at the Riding Officer on the quayside whose face was dark with rage. "I don't think you've much choice."

"You'll hang, Rudd! Count on it!" Rackam shouted.

Valentine looked back at the captain. "I'm innocent of the charges he makes against me."

Falton's face was granite. "Whatever a man has or hasn't done has no bearing on his presence on this ship. Only his actions here are accountable."

"Then I'm obliged to you, sir."

Captain Falton smiled then. "You'll not be sorry. Bos'un, sign him on and fit him out from the slop chest. If he catches pneumonia in this mild weather, then the Greenland Sea will kill him for certain. And I've no time to be conducting burials when there's big fish blowing round us."

They moved back to the waist of the ship where some of the crew were still staring shoreward at their diminishing families. Valentine spotted Billy at the edge of the crowd, waving. He was shouting but Valentine's ears were still awash.

"What's he saying?"

"My Dad says he'll let your Margaret know."

Margaret. He had forgotten all about her with nearly drowning. Her letter! He felt inside his coat and pulled out the sodden envelope. The ink had run, but he tore it open. Although smudged, her writing was still legible. He skipped through the lines until he found what he was looking for at the end. She wrote she knew he would have to stay away from Saltburn for a time, but she would wait for him, no matter how long. He smiled then. But she would be waiting longer than she thought.

Northern Star was crossing the harbour bar, butting into the swells of the German Ocean. The helm was put down and she veered West-North-West, on course for the Shetland Islands where she would fill out her crew and take on stores. When orders were called to man the braces to trim the sails, a sailor struck up a shanty, and the other hands joined in to sing the choruses.

> *"... Haul home those sheets, my hearties,*
> *With a light and pleasant gale,*
> *We will crowd aloft our sail,*
> *And we'll think on those girls when we're far far away.*
> *And we'll think on those girls when we're far, far away..."*

Valentine stood for a second, staring back at Whitby's white cottages clinging to the cliff-side, the abbey dark and brooding on the headland. Then he looked aloft at the spread of canvas, bellied now, gorging on the wind and the promise of a fair passage. Well, he had envied Jonathan this voyage. Now it looked as though he too was going to find adventure.

"Come along, lad. We'll get you togged out," the bos'un said.

"Aye, aye, sir," Valentine replied with a smile.

- THE END –